THE WHISPER OF TREES

NICHOLAS COOK

VOICE FROM THE CLOUDS

ABOUT NICK COOK

Somewhere back in the mists of time, Nick was born in the great sprawling metropolis of London. He grew up in a family where art was always a huge influence. Tapping into this, Nick finished college with a fine art degree tucked into his back pocket.

In 2006 he became a full time writer and wears two author hats these days; under the Nick Cook moniker he writes sci-fi and under Nicholas Cook he pens contemporary fiction.

Nick has many interests, from space exploration and astronomy, to also travelling this incredible planet of ours. His writing in many ways reflects his own curiosity about life and the world around him. He loves to let his imagination run riot to pose the question: What if?

Published worldwide by Voice from the Clouds Ltd.

www.voicefromtheclouds.com

In memory of all the people that we have loved and lost, but will always live on in our hearts.

What's the life of a man any more than a leaf?
A man has his seasons so why should we grieve?
Although in his world we appear fine and gay,
Like a leaf we must wither and soon fade away.
If you look in the churchyard, it's there you will see
Those that have passed like a leaf from a tree.
When age and affliction upon them did fall,
Like a leaf they did wither and down they did fall.

Lyrics from the folk song 'What's the Life of a Man'

'All the art of living lies in a fine mingling of letting go and holding on.'

Havelock Ellis

CHAPTER 1

Here under the cool canopy of leaves, it always felt as if I'd stepped into something of a dream after the everyday chaos of the modern world. The foliage above me held at bay the unusual warmth of the late-summer heatwave that had melted what was beyond the boundary of this woodland. The tranquillity beneath this green jewelled roof was almost like a slight thickening in the air. It made me slow down whenever I was here in Wytham Woods, the place that felt like home for my soul.

Birdsong echoed among the trees, the familiar heartbeat of these woods' soundtrack. Their early-morning chorus was almost raucous as the birds laid their stakes to the territories that carved the woods up. It was easily audible even over the respirator I was wearing, as I worked in this, my open-air laboratory.

Despite my mask I could still smell the rich, heady compost scent of the woods around me as I prepared my experiment. That smell was something I'd always found mildly intoxicating, like the whiff of a great whiskey.

I fastened a plastic bag around a beech sapling, then wrapped tape around them to seal in my mini greenhouse around the small tree. Finally, I made sure that the thin plastic hose was fastened securely in place.

Ever since I'd first visited Wytham, a remnant of the ancient wild woods that had once covered the whole of Britain, I'd fallen in love with it. At over four hundred hectares, the woodland was now owned by Oxford University.

The woods seemed a world away from the bustle of the city only a few kilometres east. And as much as Evie and I loved our city lifestyle, for both of us, Wytham Woods was our idea of heaven.

As I worked, a robin appeared on the tall fence surrounding my experiment and watched the silicon hose with an inquisitive eye as if it were an oversized worm. I trailed the hose to the nearby experiment cage, one of many throughout the woods. These cages housed the research work of those at the Oxford colleges and beyond. And I was one of those *beyond*, having finished my degree at Bangor University. My original career choice had been forestry, but in my final year I'd stumbled upon the cutting-edge research work of Suzanne Simard. She and her peer group were conducting revolutionary research work into mycorrhizal tree networks, more popularly known as the 'wood wide web', a much catchier title. It'd shifted how I and many others thought about trees for ever. That encounter had changed the course of my life and I'd abandoned a career in forestry to pursue this new path, where my heart now truly lay.

Realising that no food was on offer, the robin flew off with a disappointed chirp as I finished connecting the hose to the gas cylinder that contained the mildly radioactive Carbon-14. I was wearing a respirator as a safety precaution, even though this gas occurred naturally all around us – in a low enough dose to not do us any harm. It was absorbed from the air by trees and plants through photosynthesis, which was where my research work – first pioneered by Suzanne Simard – came in. Increasing the beech sapling's direct exposure to Carbon-14 would raise the amount of it absorbed by the tree. This would then act as a radioactive tracer – not the melt-your-face-off variety, but more on a luminous-clock-face level. The fingerprint of that tracer would indicate whether or not the first step of my experiment had worked.

With the cylinder now connected, I checked each of the equilibrated stem chambers – small cylindrical devices connected directly to the trunks of surrounding beech saplings. These samples would tell me more definitively whether or not my experiment had worked. I headed over to the large beech tree in the centre of the copse. It was at least a couple of hundred years old and towered over its offspring. The most important chamber was connected to this ancient tree. If the Carbon-14 trace element reached that network hub tree, then it would be like Christmas had come early for me.

That was it; my experiment was ready.

As I headed back to the cage, anticipation grew inside me. Months of preparation, including negotiating the red tape with Oxford University so I could perform a radioactive experiment within Wytham Woods, was about to come together.

I made a note on my phone of the exact time I was beginning the experiment. My heart began to pound faster as I turned on the valve of the Carbon-14 cylinder.

Hopefully this would be the start of everything I'd been painstakingly working towards.

I couldn't see it, but I could visualise the invisible gas travelling along the pipe and swirling over the leaves of the beech sapling enclosed in its plastic greenhouse.

I locked the cage to protect my experiment from any interested wildlife – and the few members of the general public that sometimes took advantage of being able to roam this woodland.

The hard part had started, and now I had to wait for up to forty-eight hours for the gas to spread through the underground fungal network.

'Hi, Adam, how's it going?' came a woman's voice from behind me.

I turned to see Evie standing beyond the high metal fence that I'd set up to keep the public away.

Quite how I'd managed to snare this gorgeous woman was beyond me. She had blown into my life on the winds of a magical spring three years ago. I had a lot to thank my oldest mate Matt for – and his wife Sarah, Evie's sister. They set me up with her after I'd mentioned how much I fancied Evie after their wedding. Before I knew it I'd been sharing a pudding with Evie on our first date at the Turl Street Kitchen restaurant in Oxford and laughing at everything. And that had been the start of all our tomorrows.

Evie wouldn't have looked out of place as a woodland elf in *The Lord of the Rings* movies. She certainly had the long, dark auburn hair, flecked with autumn fire, although her eyes were dark oak brown rather than gemstone blue. This vision of beauty now stood before me with a rucksack slung over her back, a bicycle helmet dangling from it.

I slipped my mask off as I headed out of the gate to meet her. 'Hi, gorgeous.'

She angled her body towards me and drew me in for a kiss. 'So is the deed done, Adam?'

I gently took hold of her shoulders and rotated her back to face the experiment cage beyond the fence. 'It's all set and the Carbon-14 is hopefully being absorbed by the sapling right now. All I have to do is wait for the results.'

Evie gave me her best dimpled smile. 'So you really are on your way now.'

'Maybe…but what if this first experiment is a bust?'

She shook her head. 'You see, Adam, that's your problem right there. You always imagine the worst possible outcome, even when everything suggests it's going to be fine. How many times have you told me how this mycorrhizal experiment has been run around the world?'

'Loads.'

'And how many times has the same experiment successfully demonstrated that the mycorrhizal fungal networks really do connect individual trees together into one big community?'

'All of them.'

'So there's your answer there then. Stop imaging the worst-case scenarios, lean into your fear and get ready to make history.'

'But even if this experiment pans out, I'll still be some way from achieving what I'm eventually hoping to prove here in Wytham. And, of course, this may just be a bust.'

Evie placed her hands on her hips. 'So says you. I wish you had as much confidence in yourself as I have.'

'If I could bottle that belief of yours in me, I'd drink it daily.'

She brushed my face with her hand. 'Unfortunately, I can't offer you a self-belief potion, but I can provide some rather excellent small-estate Java coffee fresh from the deli.'

'Oh, you temptress.'

'Absolutely,' Evie replied with a laugh. She headed past me and placed a hand on the large broad trunk of a nearby oak. 'Arwen, you need to have a word with your disciple here.'

I smiled at the name that Evie had come up with for the tree. Every couple had their movie and *The Lord of the Rings* had become ours. She had even christened my mycorrhizal research the language of the Ents – again, a much catchier title.

'Okay, if that tree starts talking to me, I'll definitely know I've lost the plot,' I said.

Evie's laugh lit me up, like it had on my first encounter with her – and ever since.

She ran her hands over the trunk of Arwen. 'So, old lady, what secrets have you got locked inside you that Adam's eventually going to reveal to the world?'

I smiled. 'So you really are talking to trees now?'

'You should try it. I find it so therapeutic chatting to Arwen here.'

'You do know if we want my research to be taken seriously we really should start calling her a network hub tree.'

'Where's the romance in that?' She pursed her lips at me. 'But I do approve of the other name you guys have for it. Mother tree sounds much more romantic.'

My smile widened. 'If you say so.'

'God, you're such a cold-hearted scientist. That aside, to think you are on the verge of listening to the secret whispers of trees is incredible.'

Evie had a way with words like this – an ability to take the scientific facts that were the basis of my life and turn them into poetry.

'I *may* be about listen to a mycorrhizal network. There are a lot of steps between now and that eventual end goal.'

She hugged me. 'And you're so going to succeed. You, Mr Roberts, are going to shake up the botanical world – not to mention open up the hearts and minds of everyone else to the true wonder of trees. Imagine what they could do with that revelation! You will become ecology's poster boy. No cold-hearted forester would be allowed to chop down a mother tree again. You were always destined for great things. It's one of the many reasons I fell for you in the first place.'

'Not for the untold riches that will no doubt be showered upon me for my research into the wood wide web?' I wiggled my eyebrows at her.

'That too – and your nice bum.' Evie squeezed my arse before dancing away, grinning.

'Where is that Java you mentioned?' I asked.

'Coming right up.'

I locked the gate behind me as Evie took a blanket out of her rucksack. With a flourish she shook it out and laid it flat on the ground, followed by a thermos flask and cups. Then she began rummaging deeper into her rucksack.

'What else have you got in there?' I asked, trying to peer over her shoulder.

'The stuff of your dreams.' Evie took out a stained paper bag that was dripping a golden liquid from its base. 'Bloody hell, the honey has leaked everywhere. I knew I should have put it in a plastic container.'

'You brought my favourite?'

'Unbelievably, there was half a tray of the best baklava in Oxford left.'

'And that's why you, Evie, are my soulmate. You're a star.'

She laughed. 'Oh, don't I know it. Can you deal with the baklava? I need to check my flute is okay.'

My eyes widened. 'You're working on something new?'

'Maybe. I've had this musical phrase looping through my head for a while – ever since the last time I was up here.'

'That sounds promising.'

Evie nodded as she withdrew a small wooden Chinese flute from the bag. It was covered in sticky globs of honey that were coated with the fluff that always lurked at the bottom of bags.

'That doesn't look good,' I said.

'Nothing a wet wipe can't sort out.' She unzipped a front compartment of the rucksack, withdrew a wet wipe and set to work.

I laid out a couple of napkins that I found stuffed into the bottom of the bag and set the baklava on top of them.

I gazed at Evie. 'This must be the first time I've seen you pick up that flute since finishing your music degree.'

She pulled a face at me. 'Hey, give a girl a break. I can't help it if my muse decides to check out on me for a while.'

'But he – or she, or it, or whatever – is back now?'

'Oh, my muse is most definitely a *she*. And, yes, she first appeared in these very woods the last time I was up here with you. I don't know what it is about this place, but it's like I can hear myself think here.'

'I know what you mean,' I said as I sat down, resting my back against the broad trunk of the oak behind us.

'Well, whatever magic this place weaves, it was here that the musical refrain first appeared in my head. But ever since it's been like a wild creature that I've been trying to sneak up on without spooking it.'

'You and your extended metaphors.'

'I am the queen of extended metaphors.' Evie fished out a honey-stained music sheet with a few lines of handwritten notes on it. 'Yep, I'm so using a plastic box next time.' She smoothed out the paper and laid it out on the blanket.

'So you're going to play me your opus?'

'More a catchy jingle at the moment, but hopefully it's the seed of something better. I'll play you what I have once I've refuelled with some coffee. I had a truly knackering day at the deli. A lot of the language students seem to have taken a shine to it, making it even busier than normal.'

'You work too hard at that place.'

'I have to. We have to pay the bills – at least until you attract some serious research funding, or I write a bestselling composition.'

I grimaced. 'Things will get better for us one day.'

She gave me a decisive nod. 'Of course they will.' She dropped down into a cross-legged position on the blanket and handed me one of the thermos cups.

I opened the lid and breathed in the fragrant earthy aroma of the coffee. It perfectly complemented the rich smell of leaf compost around us.

Evie raised her cup to mine. 'I'd like to propose a toast. Here's to the success of your stage-one experiment into wood wide webs – and the possibilities that will lead to.'

I clinked my cup against hers. 'And here's to the return of your muse.' I took a sip of the coffee and the flavour of deep-roasted beans overwhelmed my taste buds. 'Damn, that is good.'

Steam billowed around Evie's face as she took a sip and nodded. 'It really is. And now on to the next stage of the feast.' She handed me some of the baklava on a napkin.

I took hold of the pastry and smiled at Evie. 'You first. Open wide and shut your eyes for the full taste sensation.'

Evie snapped her eyes closed and opened her mouth, a smile curling at the corners. I reached forward towards her, honey running over my fingers, and placed the baklava on the tip of her tongue.

She began to chew and then opened her eyes wide. 'Oh my god, that's incredible.'

I licked the honey from my hand. 'So good.'

Evie reached out, wrapped her fingers around my wrist and grinned. 'No, let me.' She pulled my hand to her mouth and ran the tip of her tongue over my fingers, her eyes locking on to mine.

I felt a tension building in my groin. 'Are you deliberately trying to turn me on?'

'Bloody right I am.' Laughing, she pulled me down on top of her and began to kiss me.

I drank in the sweetness of her mouth, still tanged with honey, as her legs wrapped around my waist.

I pulled myself up and glanced around us. 'What if somebody sees?' I said.

'The footpaths are well away from here. But if you don't want me…' Her grin sharpened her feline-like features.

'Oh, don't you worry, I want you so bad it isn't funny.' I lowered myself back on to her and we kissed again. My heart accelerated as Evie pulled at my belt buckle.

My body flooded with warmth as I slid my hand down and began undoing her trousers.

Time blurred around us as we pulled each other's clothes off. Soon it was skin upon skin, the heat of the dappled sun on my back. Evie let out a small sigh as I slid into her.

We melted into each other, the world becoming hazy as the

ache built inside me. Then Evie clasped my face between her hands, her eyes finding mine, our breathing synching. Her mouth fluttered as a moan escaped her lips. She leant back, her abdomen rippling, her fingers clawing into the soil beyond the island of our blanket.

A surge of joy rushed through me as we came together, two beings fused as one for a fleeting heartbeat. No me, no her, just us. A sense that I was complete for the rarest of moments.

As our passion rolled away like thunder into the distance, we clung on to each other in a tangle of limbs. Together we looked up into the kaleidoscopic canopy of green crystal leaves gently swaying in the breeze that kissed the trees.

Those precious seconds were beyond perfect.

I propped myself on one elbow and looked down at Evie. 'God, I love you so much.'

'Me too, mister. You really are my perfect guy.'

'So if that's the case and I managed to please you, my lady, how about hearing that song of yours now?'

Evie beamed at me and rolled over, grabbing her flute, which had been pushed to the edge of the blanket.

She knelt on the blanket, a mosaic of sunlight tracing the curves of her perfect naked body. She placed the flute to her mouth, gazing down at the sheet of music. Then she closed her eyes and an immediate look of serenity filled her face.

I could already tell that she was tapping into somewhere deep within herself for this music. But when she began it was much more than anything I could have imagined.

The melody grew, a living shining thing. As the notes swirled it was like Evie was reaching into the centre of my being. Even the birdsong seemed to grow quieter, as though nature herself had been captured by its spell.

And I knew right then I was listening to something extraordinary – a lightning flash of brilliance. Too soon the notes drifted away to silence.

I became aware of the tears on my face and wiped them away. 'God, Evie, that was just amazing, but I want to hear the rest.'

She shook her head. 'Sorry, no can do. That's all I've got.' She chewed her lip as she gazed at me. 'But you liked it?'

'Evie, it's already beyond brilliant. Look at me – just a few seconds of hearing it and I'm a mess.'

Her smile reached her ears as she drew me into a fierce hug. 'I thought it might be something special, but I couldn't be sure until someone else heard it.'

I kissed the side of her neck. 'You, Evie, are going to shake the musical world up with this piece when it's finished.'

I felt her stiffen in my arms. For a second I thought I'd said something wrong.

'Turn around very slowly, Adam,' Evie whispered into my ear.

'Please tell me that we haven't got company?'

'Not in the way that you mean...'

Carefully I turned to see a deer – a doe going by her lack of antlers – gazing at us from less than ten metres away. Standing by the large oak tree, the doe's fur was the same rich gold as the baklava honey we'd just eaten.

'God, she's so beautiful,' Evie whispered, her arms still wrapped around me.

'Maybe she heard your music and was drawn here, Pied-Piper style.'

'I'll certainly settle for her rather than a load of rats,' Evie replied with a soft laugh.

The deer's head jerked to one side, its stance instantly alert. The cracking sound of twigs came from somewhere close by.

It was then that I noticed the birds had stopped singing. The magic of only a moment ago was washed away as my scalp prickled.

Before either of us could move, a large black dog emerged from the vegetation. The doe shook visibly as the dog padded towards her, its head down. The doe's muscles tensed across her haunches as she got ready to spring away.

Part of my brain registered what was about to happen and I grabbed the nearest thing to hand: my discarded boot. I lobbed it straight at the dog.

'Clear off!' I shouted.

The deer bounded away into the woods, the spell broken.

The dog turned and looked straight at Evie, not me. She shuddered just as the deer had done, as if she had become the dog's prey. I grabbed my other boot and hurled it at the beast. It ducked sideways and my boot sailed harmlessly past, but at least the animal had broken eye contact with Evie. Barking, the dog began racing away in the direction the deer had sprinted.

'I thought bloody dogs weren't allowed in the woods,' Evie said.

'They're not. Some idiot must have ignored the signs.'

'Bastards. I just hope that deer will be okay.'

'Me too. If I get my hands on the owner…'

At that moment we heard the unmistakable sound of footsteps.

'Um, Adam, before you let rip into whoever is heading this way, I'd better point out that we're still both starkers,' Evie said.

'Fuck!' I grabbed my clothes and began to haul them on as fast as I could.

CHAPTER 2

We fastened buttons and pulled up zips as the shuffling footsteps drew closer. I was hunting around for my boots in a pile of old, rotting beech leaves when an old man appeared between the trunks heading straight towards us with the help of a walking stick. The guy had a wild, curly grey beard and hair to match.

Bare-footed, heat rising in my chest, I strode towards him. 'Was that your bloody dog that just chased a deer away?'

The old man fixed me with his hazel eyes and arched his bushy eyebrows. 'Dog?' he said with the honeyed tones of a Somerset accent. 'No, nothing to do with me. Dogs aren't allowed in these woods.'

I felt my blood rapidly cooling. 'I know that. Maybe it was a stray that managed to find its way in.'

'Possibly, but stray or not it's definitely not welcome here.' Just for a moment the old man's gaze tightened on me as if he was looking *into* rather than *at* me. Then his eyes travelled away to Evie, who was hurriedly doing up her last shirt button.

If he'd sussed out what we'd just been up to, he was too much of a gentleman to say. Instead, his gaze came to rest on the flute lying on the blanket.

'Ah, so you're the source of that wonderful music I just heard,' he said.

Evie ran her hand through her hair, trying to tame her ruffled locks. 'I was trying out what I'm hoping will evolve into a new composition.'

The man's eyes twinkled as if two tiny stars had suddenly appeared in them. 'My dear woman, if what I heard is anything to go by, then you *must* complete it.'

Whoever this man was, I was already warming to him. 'I couldn't agree more.' I stuck out a hand. 'I'm Adam and this is Evie.'

The stars in the old man's eyes glowed even more strongly as he shook our hands. 'As in the first humans?'

Evie peered at him and then her expression widened. 'Oh, yes, we get that a lot!'

He smiled. 'I can imagine. Anyway, I'm delighted to meet both of you.' He gestured to himself. 'I'm Silva – with an *a* rather than *er* at the end.'

I scratched my ear. 'As in the Latin name for trees?'

Silva nodded. 'The very same. I had poetical parents.' He turned to Evie. 'So, going by the evidence of my ears, you're a composer?'

'I'm trying to be, although I've had a bit of a dry patch for far too long. I've been working at a deli in town in the meantime. Thankfully, Wytham seems to have thrown some fresh inspiration my way.'

The old man nodded. 'Yes, these old trees have been rather good at inspiring people for as long as I can remember.' Silva gestured with his walking stick towards the fence. 'Talking of inspiration, are those plastic bags tied all over my beech saplings anything to do with you, Adam? You look like one of the scientific types I often seen in my woods.'

I couldn't help but notice his proprietorial use of *my*. I often thought of Wytham as my woods too. I wouldn't have been surprised if everybody else who came here had exactly the same feeling.

'Yes, that's all my handiwork. They're all part of my research into what are called mycorrhizal networks. We're starting to discover that the root systems of trees are linked together via fungal filaments. The beech trees I'm testing have been shown to support each other, even sending nutrients to trees that are struggling to find light. Some call this the wood wide web.'

'Oh, do they now?' Silva replied without so much as a smile.

'As in the World Wide Web,' Evie said, clearly trying to prompt some sort of amusement.

Silva shrugged. 'I don't have much time for such things, however it's good to hear that people are finally catching on to the true nature of trees. They're right old gossips when you get to know them.'

Evie gave me the *here we go* look, but held back from winding her finger by the side of her head.

'So you're trying to eavesdrop on my trees then,' Silva continued.

'Pretty much,' I replied. 'My first step is to confirm the existence of the wood wide web here in Wytham. Then I hope to move on to stage two.'

'Stage two being?' Silva asked.

'I want to try to detect the electrical pulses that travel between the trees. My theory is that the mycorrhizal network also acts as a rudimentary form of nervous system in the woodland.'

Evie nodded. 'Adam's research work is breathtaking. He'd never say so because he's far too modest, but he is a bona fide genius.'

I shook my head. 'Don't listen to Evie. She's more than a bit biased.'

Silva smiled. 'That's as maybe, but I'm inclined to agree with her. It's wonderful to see someone pursuing such a genuinely fascinating route of enquiry. I'd love to know how you get on with your research work.'

'Well, feel free to swing by anytime. I'm here most days of the week.'

'Isn't that the truth,' Evie said. 'I have a hard time dragging Adam away even for a holiday, Silva.'

'I can understand Adam's passion for these woods. They are very special,' the old man replied.

'There you go, Evie. A fellow tree hugger if ever I met one.'

Silva smiled, but then my phone started to buzz inside my trouser pocket. I dug it out to see a text on the screen.

'I'll take that as my cue to bid you both a good evening,' Silva said. With a wave and doff of an imaginary hat, he turned and headed away into the woods.

'Give him a pointy hat and I'd be convinced he was Gandalf,' Evie whispered through the corner of her mouth.

I smiled as I looked at my phone screen.

Hey, guys, where are you? We've been waiting for you by the Ferris wheel for the last thirty minutes. Sarah xxx

'Damn it, I totally forgot that we were meant to be meeting up with Matt and Sarah at St Giles' fair tonight,' I said.

Evie squeezed her eyes shut for a moment. 'Oops, our bad.'

'I'll let her know we're on our way,' I replied.

Evie reached out and gently touched my arm. 'Actually, I wouldn't mind heading home instead.'

I felt a spike of concern as I noticed the greyness around her eyes. 'Are you feeling okay?'

She shrugged. 'Yeah, fine, just a bit tired. Another long shift and all that.'

'Well, we can cry off and tell her you're not feeling great.'

Evie looked at me and then slowly shook her head. 'Actually, no. You know what Sarah's like. She'd be around in a split second, whipping out her stethoscope to give me a full check-up. You know how keen she is to diagnose everything, even when it's just exhaustion. Anyway, I'm certain I'll be fine once the adrenaline of a fairground ride or three kicks in.'

'Are you really sure?' I said as I found my boots at last in among the leaf mould and began pulling them on.

'Yes, but thank you for worrying anyway.'

As I stood up she pulled my face to hers.

I smiled through her passionate kiss. 'Alternatively, we could take our naked party back home?'

She nudged me in the arm with her fist. 'And as tempting as that is, I want a toffee apple even more right now. Sorry.'

'In that case, let's go.' I presented my arm to Evie.

She did a little curtsy, grinned and took it. 'Then to St Giles', my good man, and don't dally.'

I raised my eyebrows at her as I grabbed my bag and cycle helmet. As we both set off together through the woods, I cast a sideways glance at the woman who meant everything to me.

'What?' she asked, catching me looking at her.

'Just that I love you so much.'

'Then that makes two of us.' She squeezed my hand.

I breathed in the scent of the woods, always rich and comforting. Above us the tops of trees were tinged with gold as the sun slid towards the horizon. Later I would find myself thinking back to this day. These woods and this woman were my life, my everything, and I had no idea how dramatically that was all about to change.

CHAPTER 3

We wheeled our bicycles through a sea of people until we eventually reached the church at the end of Magdalen Street. As we padlocked our bikes to the railings, the street fair was in full throbbing swing. It stretched away along the broad tree-lined street in a heaving mass of people. A riot of rival sound systems from the numerous rides and the smells of street food and exhaust fumes from the countless generators assaulted our senses.

For me the St Giles' fair marked the moment between the ending summer and the coming autumn at the end of September. Already the cooler air had taken hold of the air tonight, heralding the coming change in seasons.

This fair also signalled the beginning of the new academic year. Soon the students would be flocking back like returning migrating birds. The matching coloured backpacks of the language students who populated the colleges during the holidays had already gone for the summer.

So this vibrant ritual of a fair always felt like a celebration, a breath between the alternating town-to-gown pulse of the city. The end of some things and the beginning of others. But most important to me was that Evie adored our annual pilgrimage here. We'd never missed it in the seven years we'd been together.

Evie grabbed my hand, the fatigue that had threatened to abort this trip already vanished from her face, which now shone with fresh enthusiasm. And I knew exactly what that meant. Sure enough, she dragged me through the crowds towards the ride that towered over all the others.

'Seriously?' I said as I took in the looming white structure.

A white metal cage shot upwards like a cannonball, catapulted up into the sky by two huge bungee cords. The passengers' screams were audible even over the R & B music blaring out from the waltzer ride next to us that made my abdomen shake.

'You mean this isn't your idea of a great night out?' Evie said with a wide smile.

'As it certainly is for you, I'll just have to swallow my fear and do this.'

'Has anyone told you that you're one of the sweetest men alive?'

'I'll remind you of that when I'm barfing the remains of that baklava all over your shoes.'

She laughed as we joined the short queue for the ride. 'I'd better let Sarah and Matt know that we're here before they start ringing us.' Evie took out her phone and began to fire off a text.

'Maybe we should find them first as we're already running so late,' I said.

'Hey, you're not wriggling out of this so easily. You know I'm an adrenaline junkie and I need my fix.'

I let out a mock sigh. 'Tell me about it.'

She swung my hand in hers and performed a little hip wiggle.

The cage had been lowered back from its launch platform and two young women, looking decidedly green, grabbed their belongings and staggered off.

The guy ahead of us in the queue took one look at the women

and shook his head at his mate next to him. He dragged him away to a double-decker bus that had been converted into a mobile bar.

Evie raised her eyebrows at their departing backs as we stepped to the head of the queue. 'What a wuss.'

'He's being sensible if you ask me,' I replied as I dug my wallet out.

Evie batted my money away. 'No, this is my treat.'

'Treat? I'd happily settle for some candyfloss instead.'

'Give up already on trying to get out of this. Anyway, you'll thank me afterwards.'

'It's just as well I love you so much.'

Evie's eyes danced as she gazed at the bored woman in the ticket booth and proffered the money to her. A moment later we were heading towards the Cage of Doom.

A young guy operating the ride pointed out the official sign that announced they were not responsible for any lost belongings. Then he pointed to the basket below it where we could deposit our things. I didn't need any persuading. I'd seen way too many rides like this where loose change and even phones had been turned into projectiles, speeding away from their owners mid-ride, never to be seen again.

I wiped my clammy hands on my shirt as we stepped into the cage to sit down. The tension ridged my muscles across my shoulders as the attendant lowered the harnesses over us, pinning us into our seats.

I couldn't help but give the sturdy harness a good push to check it was locked into place.

Evie rolled her eyes at the young guy, who smirked at her.

'Is it too late to change my mind?' I asked.

'Just relax and enjoy the ride,' Evie said.

'Easy for you to say.'

A totally unnecessary countdown began over the tannoy, which only heightened my tension, complete with fast, throbbing dance music.

'Three, two, one, ignition!' a recorded male voice boomed out.

It felt as if a huge boulder had slammed into my stomach as the stretched bungee cords tethering us to the tall metal arms either side of the cage did their stuff and started to contract.

I let out a strangled yelp as the buildings of St Giles' blurred around us. I squeezed my eyes shut and clamped my hand around Evie's as a primordial scream, my last protest against my imminent certain death, erupted from somewhere deep within me.

As we began to slow, the whistling wind was replaced by the noise of the fair far below us. Evie's whoops almost drowned me out as the cage started to spin.

Then the head-rushing acceleration fell away to nothing as our chariot to the stars came to rest at the top of its catapulted arc. I felt an unexpected ache that we hadn't kept on flying up into the fading sunset.

For a brief, glorious moment we hung in perfect suspension, the view of the hidden-away quads of the Oxford colleges arranged all around us like a miniature city. A shrill cry came from the sky above us and I looked up to see a red kite, one of the bigger birds of prey, spiralling directly overhead.

'I love you, Adam Roberts!' Evie shouted out, pulling my attention back to her.

But before I could reply, the cage started to drop fast, spinning on its axis as it turned into something like a snowball gathering speed while rolling downhill.

The magic of the previous minute was swept away as my fear kicked back in. My scream impossibly ratcheted up several octaves as we hurtled towards the ground. And then, at last, the elastic began to tense again, slowing us once more and making my stomach rise to my throat. We were catapulted back up a second time and sheer unadulterated terror threatened to turn on the tap in my trousers.

In stark contrast to me, Evie's laughter grew only louder, her eyes widening.

This stuff of my nightmares continued for what seemed like hours but in reality was just a couple of minutes. And then the winches were slowly lowering our cage back to the launch platform.

My legs felt hollowed out as we stepped off the ride.

We grabbed our belongings from the basket. As we left the ride, we ran straight into Matt and Sarah, who were waiting outside, applauding us.

Matt had bits of sawdust in his hair as usual, suggesting he'd come straight from his studio. Sarah's long, blonde hair was scooped up with pins at the back of her head, the no-nonsense look of a junior doctor who'd come directly from work. She might have been less of a free spirit than Evie, but Sarah was just as warm-hearted.

'Bravo, guys,' Matt said as he slapped me on the shoulder. 'Mind you, mate, you were screaming so much that you could have given a female opera singer a run for her money.'

'Thanks for your compassion.'

Laughing, Sarah planted a kiss on my cheek. Then she wagged her finger at Evie. 'Hey, sis, how could you drag your poor boyfriend through something like this once again?'

'I just like to test out how much he loves me occasionally.'

'You guys,' Sarah said. She hugged Evie and then pulled away, her nose wrinkling.

'God, no wonder you guys are so late, I can almost smell the sex on you.'

'You can?' I blurted out before my brain had a chance to clamp my mouth shut.

Evie pulled a face at me and shook her head.

Sarah and Matt exchanged a look and then both burst out laughing.

'Gotcha! That was me just fishing,' Sarah said.

Evie shrugged. 'What can I say? Sometimes we just can't help ourselves...' She beamed at her older sister.

Matt rubbed his stubbled chin. 'You guys have been together for three years now and you're still at it like rabbits.'

'And I am so jealous,' Sarah said, raising her eyebrow at us.

'Hey, talk for yourself,' Matt said. 'Personally, I'm cool with our once-a-week sex life.'

Sarah rolled her eyes at her husband. 'Yeah, like I said, Evie, I'm so jealous.'

Sarah and Evie both snorted in unison.

These two were by far our best friends. Matt and I went way back, even going to the same secondary school together. However, the trajectory of our lives had taken very different paths from that point onwards. He'd pursued the arts, a bit like Evie. But rather than music, Matt's muse came wielding a chisel. He was a sculptor and had managed to make a decent living out of his work. He'd even taken up some forge work to help sculpt the gates that adorned many of the Oxford colleges.

Matt had come to Oxford ahead of me, having secured himself an Arts Council grant to pursue his passion. And it was here that he'd met Sarah – in A & E after he'd pulled a tendon in a rugby match. I'd known she was the one for him from the first moment I'd met her. I'd been proven spectacularly right when they were married within a year.

In my book, Sarah was the perfect woman for Matt. When he lost himself in his work, and he often did, she was the level-headed one that kept him anchored, especially when he descended into extended periods of self-doubt. Depression had always dogged Matt, but that seemed consigned to history since he'd met her.

Sarah in contrast was a rising star at the John Radcliffe Hospital in Oxford. She was a brilliant junior doctor on the cusp of choosing her medical specialism. Consultants from various departments were already all over her as they competed to encourage Sarah to join their own area. In many ways she was like

Evie: someone with a raw talent natural combined with a razor-sharp mind.

'So what do you guys want to do first now you've survived the vomit comet?' Sarah asked.

'Food, of course,' Evie said.

'Followed by a very large drink of something very alcoholic,' I added.

'Then we, your wingmen for tonight, have you covered,' Matt said. 'We've already scouted out the fair while we waited for you to join us.'

'And knowing your loves of all things culinary, if you'd like to follow us,' Sarah said.

We threaded our way through the crowds to one of the stalls set up just beneath the broad canopy of one of the large plane trees.

I'd always thought that the plane trees along St Giles' were the element that really gave this street – bordered by the college's beautiful tall stone buildings – its truly magical feel.

The smell of fragrant curry wafted up my nose as we approached the stall and despite my recent near-death experience I was immediately hungry. The stall itself had been set up by the Tree, one of the best Indian restaurants in Oxford. Their menu blackboard listed an abundance of enticing street food that made me feel even hungrier.

'I can personally recommend the bhel puri,' Matt said. 'It's like Rice Krispies with Indian attitude.'

'It sounds as if you've been here already,' Evie said.

Matt raised his shoulders. 'Hey, if you guys were late because you were too busy shagging, what's a guy to do?'

I laughed. 'Fair point.'

'Anyway, I'll happily go for a second round. It really was that good.'

Sarah patted her husband's stomach. 'This man has an endless capacity for food. Anyway, I can recommend the mulled wine from over there. I don't care that Christmas is miles away – I love me a bit of hot spicy wine.'

Evie dipped her chin towards me. 'Okay, Adam, it looks as if we have some catching up to do.'

A short while later, my stomach was filled with delicious Indian food – along with a nice whiskey from the round I'd bought at the Eagle and Child at Evie's insistence. Considering the pub was an old haunt of Tolkien and his literary friends, there was obviously no other choice for us.

Now Evie was busy herding us towards a hoopla stall. She gestured at a giant pink fluffy elephant. 'You see that one? It's so got my name all over it.'

I stepped forward. 'Then your wish is my command.'

'Get it and you'll have my undying love…and probably a good snog too.'

'If snogs from you are up for grabs, then I'm up for it,' Matt said.

Sarah gave him *the* look.

Matt grimaced. 'Or then again, maybe not.'

I bought three hoops and set to work. My first shots went wide and bounced off the back wall. My last hoop landed on the bowling pin at an angle.

I fist-thumped the air. 'There you go! One pink elephant, Evie.'

But the stall holder was shaking his head. 'Sorry, mate.' He pointed to the sign that showed the hoop had to land cleanly over the pin – and, worse still, I needed all three for the jackpot prize.

Matt slapped his thigh, pantomime style. 'Ah, no snogs for you then, Adam.'

'If you need a job doing,' Evie said. She paid for another three hoops and literally rolled up her sleeves. Evie transformed from sunny soul to the huntress, a being of pure focus. Her eyes locked on to the pin like a cat about to pounce on its prey.

It never stood a chance.

In quick succession she launched the hoops, sending them

sailing perfectly flat through the air, Frisbee style. She had judged the momentum just right. They all arced down and landed one on top of the other around the pin.

Evie punched the air before trading high fives with us as the stall holder unhooked the giant pink elephant from the roof and gave it to her with a smile.

Seconds later, Evie was singing, 'I am the champion,' to the tune of the Queen song at the top of her voice as she cuddled her elephant.

This was typical Evie – the woman who could light up my darkest days with brightness and laughter. But then I noticed the beads of sweat that were popping out all over her forehead, despite the distinct chill that was now tinging the air.

'Do you feel okay, Evie?' I asked.

'A bit hot, but I'm fine,' she replied.

A look of immediate concern filled Sarah's face as she placed her hand to her sister's forehead. 'Jesus, you're burning up, Evie.'

She sighed. 'Maybe I got a chill when Adam and I went *au naturel* in Wytham Woods.'

Matt did a comedic double take between us. 'Oh, you dirty dogs.'

'Well, missy, thanks to your creative love life you need to get back to your flat pronto. Take two paracetamol, have a warm bath and then plenty of rest. Doctor's orders.'

Evie blew her cheeks out at her sister. 'You're no fun, sis.'

'Don't make me tell you twice, young lady,' Sarah replied.

Evie snapped a salute and then hooked her arm through mine. 'Come on, you. I don't think I'm going to win this one.'

She smiled at me but I noticed the greyness around the edges of her eyes was back again.

'Let's get you home,' I said, wrapping my arm around her.

The deer rushed through the woods, her mouth wide, spittle beading her lips. The black dog was closing the distance between them fast, a shadowy wraith weaving through the trees behind her.

The doe hurtled down a ravine towards a small stream. The embankment gave way beneath her and she started to slide. Her rear legs splayed outwards, the deer trying to slow her descent, but she crashed into the water, kicking up spray.

The dog crested the embankment and paused, the hiss of its breath and the deer's panting the only sounds. The dog gazed down at the deer now floundering in the stream as she tried to regain her footing.

The beast snarled and exploded into a leap, propelling itself towards its target. The deer, desperate now, lunged towards the far embankment, her hooves scrabbling on the soft mud to try to gain purchase.

It was all the time the dog needed.

The beast crashed into her, smashing the doe to the ground. The rims of the white irises circling her huge black eyes stared up at her attacker as the dog pinned her down. Her chest rose and fell fast, a stillness descending over her as she waited for her end.

With a low growl, the dog lunged downwards and clamped its powerful jaws around the doe's throat. She didn't make a sound as the beast began to tear the flesh from her. Then only the softest sigh as her tongue lolled to the side and her life force ebbed away.

I could feel the heat and metallic taste of the doe's blood on my lips. I was the dog...

I jerked as if I'd just fallen from a great height and opened my eyes into darkness. My heart pounded in my chest as I focused on the dim room around me. Evie was curled to my side on the bed.

I pulled away the sweat-soaked sheets from my chest and took a deep gulp of air, trying to loosen the knot in my stomach.

Slowly the scientist within me rallied as I began to properly wake. It was a dream, just a dream, my subconscious playing out the scenario of that bloody dog we'd encountered back at Wytham Woods.

I forced my hands that had clenched into fists to relax. I deepened my breath, trying to loosen the buzz of adrenaline that had flooded my system. But the dream wasn't done with me quite yet. There was still the deep unease that something was wrong.

I instinctively turned to Evie and gently placed my hand on the back of her neck. She was definitely hotter than she should have been, and my concern ratcheted up.

So the fever hadn't passed despite the paracetamol she'd taken. But knowing Evie, she would still insist on pushing herself to go into work the next day regardless. I shook my head, making a promise to myself.

No, not on my watch.

Evie needed rest and I would insist on it. If necessary, I'd call out the big guns in the form of Sarah. Meantime I'd roll out cold compresses and get her to drink plenty of water.

I had to resist the urge to spoon protectively around Evie. I didn't want to heat her up even more. Instead, I settled for resting my hand gently on her shoulder as the spin of my thoughts slowed and I gradually drifted back to a restless sleep.

CHAPTER 4

I woke into the haze of a grey morning, my mind a tangle of cobwebs. As I began to surface into consciousness, fragments of the previous night came rushing back, especially that awful dream. I reached towards Evie's side of the bed to find a space where she should have been. A huge ice-cold wave of anxiety crashed over me. I sat up, now wide awake and really worried.

'Evie, where are you?' I called out, tension tightening my voice.

'I'm out here making breakfast.' Her voice carried in through the open bedroom door, her tone perfectly normal.

I pulled on my dressing gown and headed out, fastening the belt around me.

I'd half expected to see Evie snuggled under a blanket and watching morning trash TV, and I wasn't prepared for the woman who was before me.

Evie was working in the kitchen, the very picture of health, the grey pallor from her skin gone. She was cooking up a storm of a breakfast. Eggs were bubbling as they poached in a pan while she mushed up avocados with a fork. Behind her, slices of granary bread were already in the toaster.

I felt worry loosen its hold inside me. 'You certainly look a lot better than you did last night,' I said, trying to keep any hint of my near panic attack out of my voice.

'And I feel it – bright as a very shiny button,' Evie replied. She headed up to me, wrapped both arms around my waist and kissed me gently. 'Good morning, my gorgeous man.'

'Good morning, yourself.' My hand instinctively rose to her forehead but she was cool to the touch.

Evie pinched her lips at me. 'See, I told you I was fine. I just needed a good night's kip to sort me out.'

'Thank god. You had me worried there for a minute, Evie.' There was no point in telling her about my dream. It had obviously just been one of those random things the mind threw at you when it wanted to wind you up.

Evie took my hand in hers and kissed my palm. 'Has anyone told you that you worry too much?'

'Yes, you – and very frequently.'

She smiled at me. 'Well, there you go then.'

I shook my head as the toaster pinged.

'Duty calls,' Evie said, heading over towards it.

She began constructing a hipster breakfast for us: avocado toast with poached eggs on top and a few chilli flakes for a bit of kick. Her secret ingredient was a really good yellow tangy sauce that she'd discovered at the deli. Meanwhile I brewed us two cups of smoky lapsang souchong, a tea that always reminded me of campfires.

As we tucked into our early-morning feast, Evie raised her chin at the window. It neatly framed the view of Wytham Woods from our attic-room flat, or at least what I could see of it this morning.

The summit of the hill of the woods had disappeared into a mist of low-hanging grey cloud. A large group of crows was just visible as they spiralled through the fog that enveloped the trees, only heightening the sense of mystery emanating from the place.

There was something about Wytham Woods that had always seemed magical to me – an ancient woodland far older than the city it sat near. Certainly, the decision to choose this flat had in no small part to do with its great view of them.

'So this is the big day for your work,' Evie said.

'It *may* be the big day. Previous experiments into mycorrhizal networks have taken anywhere between twelve to thirty-six hours to transfer the Carbon-14 between the trees. And there is, of course, a very real chance it may not work at all.'

Evie shook her head. 'Oh, it will. I can feel it in my bones.'

'My forever optimist,' I replied.

'Hey, it's a tough job, but somebody has to take on that role in this household.' She finished the last of her avocado toast and transferred her tea to a thermal mug that she put into her bag.

I was already on my feet to challenge her. 'There's no way you're going into work after your fever yesterday.'

She shook her head. 'Adam, I'm fine. Please stop fussing.'

'Look, even if you're feeling brighter, you should at least allow yourself a day off. When was the last time you had a sick day anyway?'

'This side of never. But I feel fine. There is no way I'm not going in and dumping my workload on Kirsty. She'll have to cope single-handed if I'm not there. Besides, I'm on a zero-hours contract. I don't get sick pay. And, like always, we really need the money.'

'Yeah, I know money is tight right now, but I still don't want you pushing yourself, especially when we're talking about your health. And Kirsty doesn't hesitate to take time off when she needs to. She must have had twelve sick days already this year.'

'Sixteen actually, and more like epic hangovers rather than being truly sick.'

'So there you go. Apart from giving you an opportunity to catch up on some TV bingeing, you could also work on your composition.'

Evie narrowed her eyes on me. 'You so know how to push my buttons, but you can stop that right now. As tempting as that idea is, I feel well enough for work and I'd feel a fraud if I took time off. Those commuters need their breakfast and coffee fix to prepare them for the day ahead. It's my duty to help keep this good city running. And, as I said before, we need the money.'

I felt a surge of guilt as she slipped her coat on. She was doing this because we lived on an overdraft most of the time.

Evie must have caught something in my expression and peered at me. 'What's going on in that head of yours?'

'Look, I know you deserve better than me. Someone who makes a proper living – not a scientific dreamer who can barely scrape by. Maybe I should have pursued a financial career in London.'

Evie scowled at me. 'No, you bloody shouldn't have. Our relationship has never been about the money and it never will be. We have a great life together, Adam, and we're both pursuers of dreams. Right now it's my turn to be the major breadwinner. And when you make it big and all that money is rolling in to fund your research, then I will give up the deli job. Then I'll really get down to some serious composing, but I'm happy to wait my turn. Meanwhile just think of me as your own personal patron of the sciences.'

'You know I will never be able to thank you enough for supporting me like this?'

'What goes around, comes around. So stop beating yourself up. Just know that you, Adam Roberts, are my dream man. I wouldn't change a thing about you. Even if we do have to scrape by, we're already rich in so many ways far beyond money.'

A slow smile filled my face. 'You really are totally wonderful.'

She curtsied. 'I'm the rainbow queen of happiness and you'd better believe it. Now, I'll have to love you and leave you since I have so clearly won this argument.'

I raked my hand back through my hair. 'I guess you have, but you get so much as a sniff and you come straight home. Okay?'

'Okay!'

~

HALF AN HOUR LATER, I was kneeling by one of the nearest saplings to my mother tree, drawing off a sample from the stem chamber of the sapling nearest it. I placed my handheld scintillation counter against the sample and waited for the numbers to flash up. My heart sank as I took in the information. Only background levels of Carbon-14 radiation had been detected.

'Relax, it's still early days,' I said to myself.

'No joy so far then?' a man's voice said from behind me.

I turned to see Silva resting his hand on his stick as he gazed at me through the fence.

'Not yet, but it's still early days.'

Silva wrinkled his nose. 'And what is it exactly that you're hoping to discover with that fancy gizmo of yours?'

'I'm hoping to detect whether Carbon-14 has been transmitted from the first sapling to its neighbours.'

'Through the miser fungus networks you mentioned?'

I smiled. 'Not miser, *mycorrhizal*. You see the fungi have formed a symbiotic relationship with the trees. Fungal mycelium weave themselves into tree roots to create the wood wide web that we told you about yesterday. Just beneath your feet are kilometres of these mycelium hyphae.'

Silva gave me a knowing nod, as if to say that once again this wasn't news to him. 'Oh, you mean the underground fungus threads. Yes, there's an infinite number of those connections throughout the woods...'

My eyes widened a fraction on Silva. He really sounded as if he knew what I was talking about – white threads were exactly what the hyphae looked like. Maybe the guy had read an article about them somewhere.

'Exactly. The network is absolutely vast and very complex. And sitting at key points of the network are what Evie calls the mother trees – such as the beech tree I'm working with as part of my experiment. As her saplings fight for light and nutrients, the mother tree can help by sharing nutrients to support them through the mycorrhizal network. And as her saplings grow, they can return the favour if the mother tree starts to struggle, doing what they can to support her with nutrients.'

Silva gazed at the beech tree with a faraway look in his eyes, nodding as I spoke. 'Just so.'

'We need to save our ancients forests around the world,' I continued. I was on a roll now. Evie had frequently teased me about how preachy I got when I was discussing my favourite subject. 'I don't mean we can't ever cut down a tree again, just do it less frequently and with more consideration. We need to incentivise people not to deforest for the sake of opening up agricultural land in areas like the rainforest. And, just as importantly, we need to protect the mother trees wherever we can and their associated mycorrhizal networks.'

Silva ran his fingers through his curly grey beard. 'You certainly sound passionate about this, Adam.'

'I am. I'm hoping my work here will help strengthen the ecological message. Time is running out to be able to do something about it.'

The old man nodded. 'People could also learn an awful lot about themselves from the trees.'

'What do you mean?' I asked.

'People tend to think of themselves as something separate from nature. Of course, that is part of human existence. You become separated from your mother when the umbilical cord is cut. And you carry the wound of that separation within you for the rest of your life. So people look for ways to connect again, to feel whole, especially through their relationships. But what if all along people were actually like your beech trees here, Adam? What if they were still connected to a network and they just didn't know it?'

'What sort of network?'

'A very ancient one. You are all part of the same interconnected ecosystem that the trees also belong to. The problem is that people see themselves as separate from nature, rather than being part of it. Hence their increasing sense of isolation in your ever more technological world.'

'This sounds like something you've given a lot of thought to,' I said.

Silva chuckled. 'Oh, trust me, I have. And if your work hopes to get the ecological message out there, then I wish you every success with it.'

In the distance a crow cried out, its harsh cry reverberating through the trees.

Silva raised his gaze towards it. 'Time for me to go, Adam, but do please send my warmest regards to that beautiful fiancée of yours.'

'Ah, we're not actually engaged.'

He gave me a warm smile. 'Trust me, you will be before long.'

'I'm not sure what you're basing that assumption on.'

'Experience.' He tapped the side of his nose.

I laughed. 'Fair enough.'

The crow called out again, a rasping sound of claw on wood.

Silva doffed his imaginary cap and the mysterious old man of the woods headed off into the trees again.

I returned my attention to my samples, but despite checking several more saplings I didn't detect any rise in the Carbon-14 radioactive isotope levels. But it didn't mean it was a bust – it could take another twenty-four hours for something to appear.

I WAS EATING some soup from a flask for my lunch while gazing at a spiderweb in a hawthorn nearby when the hairs on the nape of my neck lifted up.

A low growl came from behind me.

Shit!

I slowly turned and peered around the broad trunk of Arwen. Just on the other side of the ancient oak was the same black dog I'd seen in the woods the day before…and last night in my dreams. Its jaws were open as it stared at me, its teeth bared. Its fur was the jet black of a starless night, its huge muscles tensing beneath the surface of its skin. A hell hound no less.

Fear coiled in my stomach, but I knew that the worst thing I could do was to try to make a run for it. The thing would be on my back in seconds. I had to avoid eye contact so it didn't think I was challenging it, and I knew not to make any sudden movements.

As I tried to think of a plan, the beast took another step towards me and snarled again, the deep note reverberating in the back of its throat.

This was bad, really bad. I scanned around me but there wasn't so much as a stick to defend myself with.

I almost jumped out of my skin as my phone warbled in my pocket.

'Nice doggy, just relax,' I said, slowly reaching for my phone. I could ask whoever was ringing me to send help.

I slowly took my mobile out as if I was showing the dog that the black shiny device wasn't a weapon that could possibly harm it in any way.

I risked glancing down at the screen and saw Sarah's name. That was weird in itself – it was the middle of the day so she should have been rushed off her feet at the hospital.

When I looked back towards the dog, I found myself staring into empty air. Where the hell had it gone?

I stood up and peered into the woods. There wasn't a sign of it anywhere, but I hadn't heard so much as a footfall.

Shaking my head, I pressed the call accept icon on my phone.

'Hi, Sarah. What's up?'

'Adam, you need to get yourself here immediately. Evie's just been brought into A & E.'

My bowels turned to water. 'Oh my god, what happened?'

'She collapsed at work and passed out. But before you panic too much, she regained consciousness in the ambulance on the way here. We're still not sure quite what's wrong with her, but she's having tests. Her blood work is being run up right now.'

I clenched my mobile in my hand. 'Something to do with that fever?'

'Possibly, but don't go crazy with worry yet. I'm sure her tests will come back fine. But she is spooked and needs her man by her side.'

'Tell her I'm on my way.'

'Okay, see you soon. Try not to panic in the meantime.'

Of course this was exactly what I did as I hit the call end button. A million awful scenarios wound through my head as I piled everything back into my rucksack. I slung it over my shoulder and sprinted through the woods to my mountain bike.

CHAPTER 5

I stood before Sarah in a puddle of nervous exhaustion. I'd just pedalled like an Olympic velodrome sprinter across the city to get here. Yes, so I'd almost killed myself, but it had been way faster than a taxi could have managed through the heavy city traffic.

'Okay, the first thing you're going to do is calm down,' Sarah said as she greeted me at the entrance to the A & E department of the John Radcliffe Hospital. 'Evie needs you to be the strong one. Whether she'll admit it to you or not, she's rattled by what's happened.'

'Just tell me she's going to be all right?' I said.

'We won't know that for sure until we've seen her test results. And, before you ask, I've pulled out all the stops. She's being given the VIP treatment. Her blood results should hopefully give us insight into what happened.'

I drummed my foot on the floor. 'You sound as if you think it could be serious?'

'Adam, please don't panic. It's not helpful. I'm afraid I just don't know.'

'Yes, sorry. So what do you think this might be?'

'The most probable thing is she's picked up some sort of mild virus at work – or maybe her blood sugar was low, which made her faint. What's her diet been like recently? She says she's been eating well.'

I nodded. 'Really well. We're both still on that flexitarian diet. Chicken only at weekends and vegetarian most of the week, with fish on Fridays. And, before you ask, we both make sure we're eating enough protein on our veggie days. But she *has* been working hard and taking extra shifts and early starts.'

'That could be a major contributing factor. She may just be pushing herself too hard and is simply exhausted.'

Even though that was potentially good news, I couldn't help but feel a pang of guilt. Our precarious financial position had pushed Evie to take on more work than she should have. Pursuing my research for my PhD was all well and good, but not if it came at the expense of Evie's health.

'Did anything happen at her work today that might have caused her to faint?' I asked.

'Why don't you ask her that yourself? She's in the last cubicle on the right. But please remember what I said.' Sarah reached up and squeezed my shoulder. 'I've got this, Adam. I'll get to the bottom of it.'

I patted her hand. 'I know you will.'

'Right, I'd better get back to my rounds with the consultant. He did me a huge favour letting me duck out to deal with Sarah's case so I'd better not push it. But don't worry, I'll be keeping an eye on her throughout the day. I'll catch you later.' She punched a number into the keypad to let me into the A & E ward. 'Just remember what I said.'

'I will,' I replied.

Sarah smiled at me before breaking into a run as she disappeared away down the corridor.

I made my way past the cubicles. Curtains were drawn around most of the beds, but a few had gaps in them. Through one I got a glimpse of a young boy sitting in bed with a large bloody gash on his shin. A woman who looked to be in her early thirties had a child's cycle helmet cradled in her lap. It reminded me that I'd had more than my fair share of visits to this A & E department – and had a few battle scars to prove it.

I reached the last cubicle. 'Are you decent in there, Evie?'

'I'm not sure I've ever been decent in my life,' she replied, making the man hidden behind the curtain in the next cubicle snort.

I entered to see Evie sitting up in bed. She dropped the glossy magazine she'd been reading on to the bed and raised her arms out to me.

In three strides I reached her and hugged her to me in a fierce embrace. 'Shit, you frightened me, Evie.'

'Not as much as I frightened myself,' she replied.

I pulled back and held her by the shoulders. I scrutinised her face as if I might be able to see what had caused this in her eyes. But she looked only bright, alert and very much the picture of heath.

'You look ridiculously okay.'

'I am. It just has to be one of those things. I'm sure it's nothing to worry about.'

'That's what Sarah was just saying.'

'See, listen to the experts. There's no need to freak out.'

Sarah's advice came back to me. This was Evie putting a brave face on things. And I needed to follow my part in this agreed script.

I forced a smile. 'If you say so, but can you tell me what happened?'

'I was crazy busy in the deli covering all the breakfast orders. Kirsty was off again.'

I frowned.

'I know, I know,' Evie said. 'So it was just me having to cope single-handedly to cover the usual crowd's orders. And then as though I didn't have enough to deal with, this bloody tour guide brings all these tourists in. The last thing I remember is barely being able to breathe as I plated up an order of eggs florentine. Then the world went black. The next thing I knew, there are all these concerned faces peering at me on the floor. The tour guide had already taken it upon himself to ring for an ambulance. By the time the paramedics arrived I tried to argue that I felt fine, but they insisted on bringing me in to give me a full check-up.' Evie spread her hands, palms upwards. 'So here I am feeling stupid and that I'm wasting everybody's time.'

She almost sounded as if she believed her explanation, but I knew better from Sarah.

I shook my head. 'No, this is exactly where you should be, Evie. Better safe than sorry.'

'Yeah, I know, but I can't help feeling like a fraud.'

'Well, you're not. It's important they investigate what caused this.'

'God, you sound just like Sarah. Talk about wasting hospital money.'

'No, you should be grateful for having such a great sister who can get you the VIP treatment in here.'

I relaxed a bit. Just by talking to Evie I could feel myself unwinding from the nightmare scenarios I'd been imagining. She peered at the rucksack slung over my shoulder. 'So what goodies have you brought for me?'

'I didn't exactly have much time to grab anything.'

'In that case, let's get ourselves organised. I've only been in here fifty minutes and I'm already bored out of my mind. Can you scout for some decent coffee and also get me a notebook and pencil? If I'm going to play along as a sick patient and sit on my arse all day, I can at least spend the time productively by working on my composition.'

'That's a good idea. I can catch up with some of the paperwork for my PhD.'

'Any news on the results yet?'

My heart clenched in my chest. Even though she should be worrying only about herself, she was still checking that things were going okay with me.

'No, nothing yet, but hopefully by tomorrow we'll have positive results.'

'Just as mine will be.'

Even though Evie was smiling at me I could see the echo of my own concern behind her eyes.

I nodded. 'It'll be an excuse for a double celebration.'

'You've got that right.'

IT WAS JUST AS WELL that both of us had work to do, otherwise boredom would have quickly set in. It wasn't as if we could sit and watch Netflix.

Evie spent most of the time writing musical notations in the notepad and quietly humming tunes to herself. I'd disappeared into my academic work, or at least I'd tried to. But I couldn't help but worry about what Evie's tests might come back with. The longer the delay in hearing the results, the more my worry ratcheted up. Now a dozen scenarios were playing through my head, all of them dark. Midway through the morning, a porter had come for Evie to move her from A & E. Much to Evie's disgust, she'd been wheeled down in her bed. It turned out that Sarah had given strict instructions that Evie wasn't to risk walking anywhere until we had a better idea of what we were dealing with. Sarah had also pulled some strings to get Evie into one of the private rooms instead of an open ward.

Evie had immediately luxuriated in her new surroundings, delighting in ordering from the exclusive menu that should have been for private patients only. She'd ordered enough for two and even a small glass of wine for me as she needed to be careful until we got her results back.

'I could get a taste for this lifestyle,' I said as I finished off the last of the wine.

Evie nodded. 'If you'd told me getting sick would mean being pampered like this, I would have developed a mysterious illness years ago.'

I laughed as the door opened and Sarah appeared.

'How is it going in here?' she said as she came and sat on the edge of the bed.

'I'm bearing up under all this pampering,' Evie said.

'Thank you for doing what you did to make this happen,' I added.

'Nothing's too much of a problem for my little sis. Thankfully, the hospital's financial administrator is a fan of mine so he bent the rules a bit.'

'Oh, to have friends in high places,' Evie said.

'Exactly. Anyway, tell me how you're feeling now,' Sarah said.

'Great, actually. I'm embarrassed to say that the more I think about it, the more I'm sure it really was just a fainting fit.'

'Let's leave the conclusions to Sarah,' I said.

'Hey, this is my body. I think I'm best placed to judge how I'm feeling.'

'We'll have to see about that,' Sarah replied.

'Absolutely,' I agreed. 'Sarah's the one in charge here, not you, Evie.'

Evie poked her tongue at me. I ignored it and turned to her sister. 'So, any news on those blood results?'

Sarah's face became serious.

My pulse sped up. She had news.

Evie didn't so much as blink, but her fingers sought out mine.

I massaged the back of her hand as I held my breath, mentally bracing myself for whatever we were about to hear.

'Oh god, will you look at you two? My cross face must look

too similar to my bad news face, sorry. It's only that some idiot in the lab has lost your blood work after their computer system crashed. So we're going to have to run the tests again.'

Evie groaned and dropped her head back on to the pillow, staring up at the ceiling. 'And how long is that going to take?'

'Unfortunately, they've switched over to the night shift in the lab now, which means they have minimal people down there. So even if I escalate your case, it's unlikely that we'll have your results until morning.'

'Bloody hell, I'll go out of my mind if I hang around here any longer,' Evie said. She dragged her teeth over her bottom lip. 'So how about this? Rather than me taking up a valuable hospital bed overnight, how about letting me head home instead? You can call me tomorrow when you get the results in and I'll come straight in if it's something bad.'

Sarah frowned. 'As your doctor, sister and friend, I'd be happier if you stayed here in case it turns out to be something more serious than you overdoing it at work.'

'I'm with Sarah on this,' I said.

'Oh, come on, guys. Look at me! I'm fine. And if it is something scary, twenty-four hours isn't going make any difference. Besides, I'll sleep a lot better in my own bed.'

Sarah twisted around and grabbed Evie's chart from the end of the bed. She began scanning through it and her expression brightened. 'Well, all your stats look great. Blood pressure is nice and healthy, you have good heart rate and your oxygen saturation levels are perfect too.'

'So, in other words, I aced my tests.' Evie put her hands together. 'Please let me go home and I promise I'll be on my best behaviour. No going into work tomorrow or anything. All I'll do is rest.'

Sarah unhooked the stethoscope around her neck. 'Let me just run some final checks on you and then we'll see.

Evie beamed at us and punched the air.

CHAPTER 6

We were at home the next morning, waiting for Sarah's call. The phone eventually rang while we were having a late breakfast, after Evie had slept in. She almost sprinted across the room to grab her phone from the sofa.

'So just tell me my results already,' Evie said before Sarah had had a chance to say a single word.

I took a large gulp of coffee as if it were a stiff drink. Evie's brow furrowed as Sarah replied. I pointed to the speakerphone icon, but Evie shook her head.

The blood began to pound in my ears. It had to be bad news and Evie didn't want me to hear so she could serve it up to me in a sanitised version. I was already anxious enough, so when Evie's face fell it was as if the Earth had shifted on its axis beneath my feet.

'Okay, I'll talk to you later,' Evie finally said. She pressed the call end button and put the phone down on the table.

I stared at her as my throat constricted. 'It's bad news, isn't it?' I squeezed out the words.

Evie blinked at me, her expression clearing. She shook her

head. 'Actually, it's annoying news. It turns out that the lab is still working through the backlog after the IT problem and they haven't got to my tests yet. Sarah said she's going ring me as soon as the results come in.'

'Oh, bloody hell, the wait is killing me.'

Evie breathed through her nose and then painted on a reassuring smile. 'Try to relax. We know the most likely thing is the results will be clear. And a good night's sleep has done me the power of good. You can see that?'

'I can…'

'So here's my plan. It's a beautiful day out there so why don't we go up to Wytham? I can work on my music while you do your thing with the saplings? We can treat ourselves to a taxi. The driver can drop us off in the car park at the bottom of the woods and it's only a short walk to your experiment site from there. I could certainly do with some fresh air.'

I rubbed my chin. 'I'm not sure…'

'Oh, come on. Otherwise we'll drive ourselves crazy here waiting for the phone to ring. At least this way we'll both be distracted doing something useful and I won't be able to overdo it under your watchful eye.'

It was hard to argue in the face of her unrelenting logic. 'I guess that could work…'

Evie bent across the table and gave me a big smacker on the lips. 'I knew you'd see sense.'

I breathed in her scent of vanilla and hoped this was the right call.

I WAS BUZZING with anticipation as I ran the Geiger counter over the leaves of the sapling about a metre away from the one contained within my improvised greenhoused tree. It emitted the most beautiful sound in the world: a series of sharp clicks.

'Bloody hell, does that mean the tree is now radioactive?' Evie said, standing next to me, both of us wearing breathing masks.

'Not at a level to do us any harm, if that's what you're worried about?'

'Nope, not at all, but this is a good sign, right?'

'A fantastic sign. But now we need to see just how good it really is.' I held up my scintillation detector to the large syringe attached to the chamber I'd connected to the narrow trunk. The numbers started to tick up on the display.

'Okay, we've just headed past the natural background level of Carbon-14 – around one point one seven for Wytham Woods, based on measurements I've taken previously. With the additional Carbon-14 the ground zero sapling has absorbed by now, we're looking for levels of five or above...'

The counter ticked up past level three.

Evie rested her chin on my shoulder as she witnessed the results come in with me.

'Come on, you can do it...' she said.

My heart lifted as the number ticked up past five. I held my breath as it rose almost all the way to six. I let out a long gasp as I stared at it, hovering just below six, not quite daring to believe it.

'Okay, don't keep me on edge,' Evie said, pulling me around so she could peer up into my masked face. 'Does that mean what I think it does?'

I grinned as my body went slack. 'The results are more than I could have hoped for. This basically proves that the Carbon-14 has been successfully transferred via the mycorrhizal network to at least this tree next to it.'

Evie whooped and hugged me. 'Oh, Adam, I'm so excited for you. That's the best news. So you're ready for phase two now?'

'Almost, but first I need to take readings from the rest of the test saplings and also the mother tree. I need to find out how far the extra Carbon-14 has spread. Then I need to model that into my computer data to give me a clearer idea of the mycorrhizal network beneath our feet.'

'Then you can really get going with shaking up the world?'

'Hopefully. Now we know that mycorrhizal networks exist here in Wytham Woods, I want to try to measure the electrical impulses that are spread through this network. If I manage to filter that out of the background noise, we really will begin to listen in to the language of the Ents.'

Evie beamed at me. 'God, this is so exciting.'

'I have a prototype detector with me, so all I need to do is connect it to the mother tree, as logic would suggest that will be the greatest source of any electrical activity. If I pull this off, Evie, then I'll almost certainly be able to attract some proper funding for my research. We might soon be in a position for you to give up working at the deli and concentrate on your music full-time.'

'This day just got a whole lot better. We really should be celebrating this with a bottle of bubbly.'

'We're not there yet, but this is a huge step forward, Evie. You're right – we should celebrate this milestone. Let's do that as soon as you've been given the all-clear from Sarah.'

Evie's expression fell. 'I'd forgotten about that for a moment.'

I grimaced and raised my shoulders. 'Sorry, that was really inconsiderate of me.'

She smiled at me. 'Adam, you could never be inconsiderate even if you tried. Right, I'm going stop interrupting you so you can get on with collecting the results from the rest of your saplings. I'll be resting under Arwen and losing myself in my music for a while.'

'Then you go and conjure up your muse.'

'Oh, don't you worry, I intend to – even if I have to tie her to one of your trees.'

I smiled at Evie and kissed her forehead.

I'D SLOWLY WORKED my way through the saplings, measuring each in turn, and the results had been just as promising as the first. The biggest surprise of all was the readings of the mother beech tree itself, which recorded almost eight. But when I thought about it, that made a lot sense. The network hub tree was linked to all its offspring, so naturally it would contain the highest density of Carbon-14, especially being the biggest tree.

While I worked, Evie sat cross-legged on the blanket at the base of Arwen, leaning her back against it as she worked on her composition. Every so often a flurry of notes would escape the end of her flute and weave their way up into the canopy of leaves.

In many ways I'd never felt so at peace as I did at that exact moment. I was doing what I loved and I knew at last that I really was on the right track. And Evie was doing what she'd been born to do: writing music that spoke to people's souls. I kept finding myself welling up as the small fragments of her music touched something deep within me.

The growing warmth of the day wrapped around us like a gentle Mediterranean sea. There was not a person to be seen or heard anywhere in the woods. Even that damned dog had stayed away. It was like we were in our own bubble where nothing could touch us.

As I took the last reading, I realised I hadn't heard Evie playing for a while. I headed out of the gate and slipped off my mask as I walked over to Arwen.

Evie had curled up on the picnic blanket under the shade of the mother tree and was fast asleep. She looked serene, like a character from a fairy tale fallen into slumber in an enchanted wood. My very own sleeping beauty.

After I'd packed away my laptop, I hadn't the heart to wake her. Evie looked so content as she slept. Dappled light played across her figure, igniting the autumnal colours of her hair. God, I loved this woman so much.

Birdsong softly echoed through the woods and I felt my brain slowing down to the deep rhythm of nature. It was then I realised just how tired I was. It seemed it wasn't only Evie who'd found the last twenty-four hours draining. I laid down next to her, wrapping her gently in my arms to spoon up against her body. Listening to her gentle breathing and the murmur of birdsong, I fell asleep.

~

I HEARD MUFFLED words as I woke. The air caught in my throat as I took in the transformation of the woodland around the still sleeping Evie and me. The trees were glowing with golden light. But that wasn't all. Beneath the deep layers of dead leaves, I could see pulses of light firing through the root systems woven together beneath the ground – as if I'd somehow developed X-ray vision.

Vertigo spun within me as I struggled to make sense of what I was seeing.

A figure was walking towards me, haloed with sunlight so bright I could barely focus on who it was. But then it came into focus and I recognised the outline of Silva, yet much younger, with a wider gait in his steps, his hair the coppers of tree trunks threaded with the greens of moss. He approached us with a wide smile on his face.

'My god, what's happening, Silva?' I said.

'I wanted you to see what is normally hidden to human eyes – the flow of life between the trees throughout the woods.'

I stared at him. 'This is the mycorrhizal network?'

Silva smiled. 'Indeed it is.'

'But how is it even possible for me to see this?'

'Because this is my gift to you, Adam Roberts.'

'Gift? I don't understand.'

'I realise that, but unfortunately our time is short and you need to listen to me very carefully. You need to be strong for what lies ahead. There is something you need to see that will help you on the dark journey upon which you're about to embark.'

'You're not making any sense.'

'But I will soon, Adam, especially when you examine Evie.'

I turned to look down at Evie still curled up fast asleep at the base of Arwen's trunk. It was then that I saw what was buried beneath her. Evie had her own hidden root system linked to her body that burrowed into the ground, every tendril blazing with light. And the tips of those roots were woven into the gossamer threads of the mycorrhizal network around her. Through it, wider arteries of luminance spidered, connecting her directly to Arwen's root bowl.

I gaped. 'But that's impossible, Silva. Evie looks as if she's wired directly into the wood wide web.'

There was no reply.

When I turned back to Silva, he had vanished.

But then his voice came through the woods, an echo on the breeze. 'Remember what you have witnessed here and let that give you the strength you need to continue.'

I felt someone shaking me. My eyes snapped open to see Evie peering down at me with her finger pressed to her lips.

A thought coalesced in my mind… It had been another vivid dream. But even as I felt relief, I also had a niggling feeling that it might be something more.

Evie spoke, pulling me back to the present.

'Be very quiet and look over there,' she whispered.

I slowly raised myself on to my shoulder, rolled over on the picnic blanket and looked across to where she was indicating. I had to stifle a gasp.

The doe from before was standing there eating some bracken – next to a large stag with huge antlers.

'Aren't they just beautiful?' Evie whispered.

After the intense dream, this was almost overwhelming. My subconscious had served up something spectacular, which had shown Evie was linked into the woods. Did that mean that these deer and I were too? Silva had said it was a gift and maybe it was.

Had it been a flash of inspiration? Maybe what I'd glimpsed was part of a much larger truth. But what did that mean?

I squeezed Evie's shoulder. 'So beautiful,' I replied.

We both drank in the truly magical moment that nature had dropped into our laps. The minutes stretched onwards and I didn't want this experience to end. But then, like the warning cries of one of Wytham's birds, Evie's phone warbled out its ringtone.

At once the heads of both deer shot up, their eyes locking on to us. Then they were bounding away fast into the trees.

Evie didn't say a word. She was staring at her phone screen, chewing her lip. She angled the screen towards me.

Sarah was displayed as the caller. Evie put the phone on speaker.

'Hi, Evie, I need you to get yourself back to the hospital as soon as possible.'

I suddenly found it hard to swallow.

'You've got the results?' Evie said in a quiet voice.

'Yes, and I need to see you to talk you through them.'

'Not on the phone then?' I asked.

'No...'

A sour taste built at the back of my mouth.

'Shit, this sounds like bad news, Sarah?' Evie said.

'Like I said, I don't want to discuss anything until you get here.'

'Cut the crap!' Evie said, her tone suddenly harsh. 'We all know that will just draw this out. So rip the plaster off and tell us right now.'

Sarah paused at the other end of the line. 'Evie, your results suggest you have acute leukaemia.'

The phone tumbled from Evie's hand as she turned to stare at me, her hands covering her mouth.

I pulled her to me, desperate to stop the world moving forward as our lives fell apart and everything we knew began to crash down around us.

CHAPTER 7

Life has the tendency to lull you into a false sense of security, leading you to believe things would continue as they were for ever. But all it takes is one major event to come out of the blue and the trajectory of your life will change completely. And that was exactly what happened from the moment of that awful phone call from Sarah.

We'd gone straight in to see her at the hospital in a state of shock. After more tests, including a bone marrow sample, it was confirmed that Evie's results showed highly raised levels of mutated white blood cells and lymphocytes. These were the warning signs that the acute leukaemia was well advanced and had a serious hold on Evie's system.

Just as unsettling as anything else was the disappearance of Sarah's professional detachment. Tears had run down her face as she'd told us what treatments lay ahead for Evie. That had been the first of so many tears as we told family and friends. On some days it felt there were enough tears to flood Oxford to the top of its tallest spires.

'I am going to fight this with every fibre of my being,' Evie had said to Lilly and James when she had broken the awful news to her parents that first week.

From then on, Evie was the eternally positive one, even in the face of our first meeting with the consultant, Dr Reece.

We'd been introduced to the senior consultant by Sarah. The doctor was a woman in her late forties with swathes of blonde hair tied back with a clip. She had the eternally kind face of most empathetic doctors.

Sarah had told us that Dr Reece was the best of the best and that she would be handling Evie's case from there on out. The experienced doctor had certainly turned out to be our anchor in the storm with her no-nonsense approach that was tempered with warmth and kindness.

From that very first meeting, which Sarah had insisted on joining, a plan was put together to attack Evie's blood cancer. The first bit of good news was that as a woman in her late twenties she was still relatively young, something that Evie latched on to. She had a strong chance of coping well with the battery of treatments the hospital was about to unleash on her. If everything went according to plan, not only did Dr Reece hope to stop the progress of the leukaemia, but actually reverse it.

So Evie had embarked on her journey of treatment, from targeted radiation therapy to toxic doses of chemo that made her as sick as a dog. But throughout everything that was thrown at Evie she remained strong and I loved her all the more for it.

'Hey, I still got my hair,' she told me after the fifth chemo treatment, yet again putting a positive spin on things.

The year crawled into the depths of winter and three months after our first appointment we were once again sitting in the waiting room of the outpatients department for a meeting with Dr Reece and Sarah to discuss progress.

Evie sat next to me, working on her musical composition in her notebook, as she always did whenever she had a moment.

I clutched my coffee, staring straight ahead at the cheerful murals on the walls that I knew far too well by now. I was looking forward to when I could consign their memory to history. The room had been decorated for Christmas with a reasonable-sized tree adorning the desk at reception and oversized baubles hanging from the ceiling.

Around us the room was filled with other leukaemia patients. Some of the woman wore headscarves to disguise their loss of hair. Yes, they looked tired and exhausted, but it was hard to ignore the strength and spirit of many of them too.

Cancer might have been one of the things that people feared most in life, but perversely it also seemed to be the thing that made the human spirit shine brightest too. The irony of it was the great suffering I saw hidden in the gazes of those who accompanied the patients. The hardest thing to watch was someone with a terminal diagnosis being stolen away bit by bit by the big C.

Evie, who'd also been scanning the people in the waiting room, whispered to me. 'That poor woman.'

I turned to see a young woman trembling and biting her lip as she stared at her hands cradled together in her lap. The older man with her who had a grey chemo-induced complexion, had his arm cradled protectively around her and was talking to her with soft comforting tones.

Right there was the dichotomy of this situation. The stoic expressions of the sufferers actually dealing with cancer were in stark contrast to the hollowed-out faces of those who loved them. I'd seen it frequently on my own face in the mirror.

'She looks on the edge of tears,' Evie whispered.

I resisted the urge to say, *And how do you think I'm doing?* Instead, I just nodded. 'Yes, she's obviously really struggling.'

Evie cuddled into my shoulder. 'Well, she needs to take a leaf out of your book. You have been my superstar. I couldn't have got through these months without your strength to lean on.'

I almost felt like sobbing myself at hearing that. I'd done everything I could to remain positive on the outside and keep my fears hidden deep within me. Evie's words only made me more determined to keep my fear from her. And it wasn't just me that was acting this way around Evie either.

When we'd had Sarah and Matt over for dinner, together with some other friends, Matt had been stoic to her face, even though I knew he was badly cut up about what was happening to Evie. But rather than veer away from the subject of death he had joked with her that he would immortalise her in one of his sculptures and sell it for a fortune to one of the galleries when she was gone. Far from being crass, his humour had been refreshing, especially when friend after friend around that dinner table had started to break down, wrapping their arms around Evie and sobbing into her neck. Later that evening she'd said to me after everyone had gone, 'Bloody hell, dealing with other people's grief is worse than even the bloody chemo!'

As we waited for Evie to be called, she ran her fingers over the back of my palm. 'You really should have brought a book with you, Adam. You must be bored out of your mind.'

'No, I'm good. I can't concentrate on anything while we're waiting. I swear that time runs at a slower rate to the rest of the universe in here.'

'I know exactly what you mean. But what about when we're not here?'

I turned to look at her. 'What do you mean?'

'You haven't looked at your research or been back to Wytham Woods since we got that phone call from Sarah three months ago. I know I've said it before, but you shouldn't be ignoring all of your own stuff for me.'

I cradled her hands in mine. 'Evie, you are my number-one priority. Nothing else is more important than that.'

'But you do know that nothing would make me happier than seeing you do what you love to do, right?'

'Yes, but I'm sticking to you throughout this and that's the end of it.'

'You can be so bloody stubborn, Adam.'

'I know, so get over it already.' A grin tugged at the corners of my mouth.

She pulled me in and kissed me. 'God, I adore you.'

At that moment, Sarah appeared in the doorway of one of the consulting rooms that lined the far wall and beckoned towards us. 'Hey, guys, we're ready for you.'

As always, I scanned her face, trying to interpret her expression, but I couldn't tell anything. After her tears in that first consultation, Sarah had been the model of professional calm.

Dr Reece stood up to greet us as we entered. 'It's good to see you both again.' She gestured to the chairs for us to sit.

Evie adjusted the collar of her cardigan as though it was chaffing. 'So how is it looking, Dr Reece?'

The consultant angled her monitor slightly towards us so we could see the screen.

'The good news is that all your scans still show that there are no secondary cancer sites appearing, but it gets trickier from here.' Dr Reece nodded to Sarah.

Sarah blinked rapidly as she leant forward in her seat. 'Evie, I'm afraid your lymphocyte counts have continued to rise despite the targeted radiation and your last bout of chemo. If your condition continues at this trajectory, it is only going to be a matter of time before it spreads to secondary sites.'

I found myself struggling to breathe.

Evie was already looking at me, her hand rubbing my arm. 'Adam, relax. It's going to be all right.'

I took a breath to force my panic back down. Let that out now and I wouldn't be able to stop the tears. And that was exactly what Evie didn't need right now.

Dr Reece was leaning forward in her chair too. 'I know what a shock it must be to hear this, but we're not out of options yet. To start with, you have a major champion fighting your corner in the form of your sister, Evie. Sarah has worked non-stop to reserve a place for you in a very promising new drug trial. But I'll let Sarah explain it to you.'

My eyes locked on to Sarah's. 'Please, anything to stop this nightmare.'

Sarah nodded, her eyes full of compassion. 'Have either of you heard of targeted genome therapy?'

Evie nodded. 'Yes, I've watched a couple of TED Talks about it since I was first diagnosed. It sounds like a really promising line of research.'

'It is. And the initial results for the first trial had an incredibly impressive eighty-five per cent recovery rate. Fifty per cent are in complete remission.'

I clasped on to Evie's hand. 'Oh my god, you mean this might actually save Evie?'

'Yes, there is a real chance it could,' Sarah said. 'Mind you, there are some quite major side effects to the treatment itself.'

'Worse than chemo?' Evie asked.

Dr Reece shook her head. 'Nothing is worse than chemo.'

Evie held the consultant's gaze with hers. 'Then I can handle it.'

'Don't forget there is a chance this trial might not work for you,' Dr Reece said.

'Eighty-five per cent success rate – I'll take those odds.' But then Evie raised her face again to reveal the tears running down her cheeks. 'How am I ever going to be able to thank you enough for this, Sarah?'

'By getting better.'

Relief flooded through me then, unlocking every muscle in my body. I welled up, unable to stop the tears that had been threatening.

Evie was immediately kneeling before me. 'Hey, Adam, but this is great news.'

I smiled at her through a kaleidoscope of tears. 'Why do you think I'm crying?'

Sarah glanced at Dr Reece. 'Permission to hug the patient and her partner?'

Dr Reece smiled. 'Permission granted.'

Sarah crossed to us and pulled us into a tight hug. 'You guys!'

And the three of us became one huge mass of emotion. As we finally broke away, Dr Reece handed us a box of tissues to wipe our eyes.

It was then that we spotted it had started to snow outside.

Evie beamed at us. 'Oh, now that's just magical – and somehow perfect too.'

I clasped my arm around her shoulders as the four of us gazed out at the large flakes drifting down, beginning to transform the normal world into one of enchantment.

CHAPTER 8

According to the poem by Emily Dickinson, hope is the thing with feathers that perches in your soul. If that was true, by the time a few months had passed Evie and I had enough feathers between us to create an eagle.

The gene-targeted therapy had been a spectacular success. Yes, the side effects of the treatment hadn't been much fun for Evie, including skin rashes and awful bouts of diarrhoea. But she had been stoic throughout her ordeal, continually pointing out to me that it was nothing compared to chemo. When Dr Reece and Sarah had told us that Evie's leukaemia had not only halted but had started to reverse and was well on its way to full remission, our combined whoops had been heard through the shut door of the consultation room.

Ironically, it was only then that my exhaustion decided to manifest itself, although not surprising as I'd finally let myself relax. I'd gone into a crash dive with a serious case of flu and couldn't look after Evie. But Lilly and James stepped in, temporarily moving from their house in Dorset to rent a flat in Oxford so they could be nearby to help Evie over the final hurdle of her recovery. Sarah and Matt did everything they could to help us too, offering help both practical and emotional in a thousand different small but important ways.

After I'd recovered, Evie's parents decided to stay and Lilly let slip that it had been Evie's idea for them to come and help. When I tackled her about it, she'd just crossed her arms and launched into a lecture about how she'd had plenty of time for her own passion project and I needed to do the same. Then she had gestured towards Wytham Woods through our attic window.

So that was how I found myself once again in Wytham Woods a couple of months after Evie had started her treatment. Spring had begun to rear its head and snowdrops had given way to the first splashes of yellow celandine and the whites of wood anemone. I picked my way among the trees, breathing in the rich compost smells like the scent of an old friend.

A raptor shriek came from above me and I glanced up to look between the green diamonds of leaves. I spotted the silhouette of a red kite skimming over the treetops, barely flapping its wings. I watched it glide away, the sentinel of the woods and sky on its forever vigil.

God, I'd missed this place.

Anticipation was buzzing inside me like a swarm of honey bees as I approached my fenced-off experiment area. But the first thing I noticed was my original test sapling still covered with a plastic bag reduced to brittle twigs. Starved of air, the life had been leached out of it. I'd been in such a rush the last time I'd been here to get to the hospital with Evie that I hadn't had a chance to remove its artificial greenhouse.

As I pulled off the polythene, a branch snapped off in my hand. I felt a pang of guilt at killing my test subject while its surrounding peers all appeared to be thriving.

I began to examine the other trees. They were all still connected to the stem chambers, which suggested that neither man nor beast had tampered with any of them. I breathed out with relief.

I headed towards the mother tree, its branches spread almost protectively over its nearest children, although of course that shade also starved its saplings of light.

I examined my prototype sensor box and wasn't surprised to see the battery sensor light was unlit. The unit was designed to only run for a few weeks unattended on its rechargeable power supply and that would have been long ago exhausted. But there was a reasonable chance that the unit had still recorded the data to its flash memory before the power had failed.

I unhooked the probe sensor from the tree and popped open the battery compartment. Anticipating the dead battery, I'd brought a charged one with me and swapped it over. At once the LED glowed red, a very good sign. Now to find out if it'd captured any data at all before the unit had died.

I connected a USB cable from the device to my laptop and at once a message flashed on the screen: *Electric sensor detected.*

Okay, so far so good. But whether the experiment had worked at all was another matter. There were a hundred things that could have gone wrong, not least that my theory of electrical impulses was completely spurious.

I almost felt breathless as I opened up the software and clicked on the import button, selecting the sensor as the data source. A moment later a bar chart appeared, showing a series of peaks and troughs. A cautious sense of relief surged through me. The unit had certainly read something, but what exactly? It was then that the bar at the very far left of the chart caught my attention. It was at least five times higher than all the rest. Curious now, I switched the chart to a sine-wave display and saw a series of rapid peaks in quick succession. According to the scale on the side, it had reached several hundred volts of power.

I sank back on to my haunches, looking up at the large beech tree. *What does that mean?*

The data suggested there had been a spike of electrical activity immediately after I had connected the sensor to the mother tree – the last time I'd been here.

There had to be a logical explanation for this.

I began to think through what could have caused such a massive spike in electrical activity. A natural phenomenon like a lightning bolt, but there hadn't been any storms that day. So could it have been linked to the Carbon-14 experiment itself? I couldn't see how exactly, but then I was entering uncharted research waters here. The more prosaic explanation was that it had simply been a glitch in the sensor before it had settled down.

Silva's voice came from behind me. 'Hey, Adam, long time no see.'

I turned to see the old man leaning on his stick – the real thing rather than a dream version.

My chest expanded at seeing my friend. 'Too long, Silva.'

'Indeed it has been. I've been keeping half an eye on your experiment, checking one of the woods' magpies didn't decide to steal one of your shiny devices fastened to my beech trees. Anyway, how are you and that beautiful lady of yours?'

'We're doing better now.'

Silva tilted his head a fraction to one side.

I raised my shoulders. 'It's a long story. The highly abbreviated version is that Evie had a major thing going on and has been having treatment to combat it.' As always, I avoided using the big C word whenever possible. I didn't like the huge reaction it created in people and I'd had enough of those to last me a lifetime.

Silva grimaced. 'I'm so sorry to hear that, but things are better now.'

I couldn't help but notice that it wasn't a question but a statement.

'Actually, yes,' I replied. 'Evie's been on a clinical trial for a new drug and it's had an incredible impact. Touch wood –' I leant over and patted the mother beech tree – 'she's on target to make a full recovery.'

'I see...' Silva made a show of looking at my laptop screen, almost as if he was trying to change the subject. 'Is this something to do with the experiment you've been running up here?' he asked.

'Yes, the start of phase two. I'm beginning to eavesdrop into those electrical impulses I told you about that travel through the mycorrhizal network. Believe it or not, the experiment seems to have worked.'

'Of course it did,' Silva replied.

I was touched that the guy had such faith in someone who was really still just a stranger.

Silva reached out and placed his hand on the trunk of the beech mother tree too. 'And what secrets did you learn from her?'

'Something curious just after I first attached the sensor. There seems to have been a massive power surge. Nothing else was recorded like it until the battery on the unit eventually ran out.'

'Oh, now that is very interesting. Any idea what could have caused it?'

'None whatsoever. But like any good scientist I'll try to replicate the results. The next stage is to extend both the Carbon-14 tests and my new electrical sensors farther throughout the woods. Then I should be able to create a map of the mycorrhizal network, and with the sensors in place I really should be able to listen in to the language of the Ents – although what they're saying to each other is anyone's guess.'

'Probably about nutrients, if I know trees,' Silva replied.

I laughed. 'Probably.'

He gestured with his stick towards Arwen behind me. 'Make sure you hook up that oak. She's one of the oldest trees in the woods and will have a lot to say.'

I smiled. 'I'll make sure I do that.'

Silva peered at me, those tiny stars shining in his eyes. 'Adam, I really am so pleased for you.'

'Thank you. It certainly feels like a major step forward. And I have a feeling that when I roll out a larger-scale version of this experiment the results will change everything.'

'Oh, they will,' Silva replied with a wide smile.

~

IT TURNED out that my prediction was the understatement of the year. With the notable exception of the electrical spike, I'd gone on to not only replicate my first results but build upon them too. Soon I had a network of sensors throughout the woods showing a definite flow of electrical activity throughout the mycorrhizal network of the trees. When I published a tentative paper, it quickly caught the attention of the world and offers of funding soon flooded in. Unexpectedly, I was even offered a lecturing job at Oxford University, which I'd happily taken. With that, our precarious financial situation had been transformed.

Alongside that, Evie had made a spectacular recovery thanks to the targeted therapy. She'd finished her course of treatment and the leukaemia had gone. Her days were filled with her music as her symphony inched towards the completion of the final fourth movement.

All this had only sharpened our appreciation for everything. We'd never been so happy.

We'd just got back from a meal out with Sarah and Matt at a new fancy fusion restaurant in Oxford. We crashed on to the sofa to watch another episode of the latest crime series we were devouring. *A Litter of Bones* featured a brilliantly surly Scottish detective and we were addicted.

As we watched, I kept catching Evie casting me sideways glances.

I finally turned to her. 'What?'

At once her expression sharpened. She had something important to tell me.

I hit pause on the TV remote and pulled myself upright. 'Oh god, what is it? Tell me you've been feeling okay?'

Evie raised her hand and cradled my face. 'Yes, I'm fine. I just love you so much. And I've got a question for you.'

Something in her smile made my heart leap. 'If you're about to propose, this is not quite how I imagined it. On top of a mountain maybe, but not curled up on our sofa.'

'No, not that, but really you should get your skates on before some other hunk sweeps me off my feet.'

I laughed. 'Noted. So what then?'

'Well, this is also something just as life-changing…' She chewed her lip.

'Okay, you're starting to freak me out now. Tell me!'

She started to trace a circle on the back of my hand with her finger. 'I was wondering if you, Adam, would like to make a baby with me? Sarah has done the tests and despite the chemo I'm still fertile.'

I stared at her, probably doing a reasonable impression of a deer caught in headlights.

Evie hugged a cushion to herself. 'Oh, great. Not quite the reaction I was looking for.'

I held up both hands to placate her. 'You caught me off guard. Just give me a moment to process this…'

She swung her legs off the sofa and started drumming her feet on the floor. 'And?'

The idea grew rapidly, like a seedling in my mind. I could picture me pushing our child on a swing, the magic of Christmas mornings, going for walks in Wytham Woods together. A slow smile filled my face.

'Does that mean what I think it does?' Evie asked.

'Yes, I think it's an amazing idea. But do you really think we're ready to be grown-ups?'

'I couldn't be more certain of anything,' Evie said. 'I love you to bits and I can't think of anything more wonderful than having a child together now I've been given the all-clear. And wouldn't we have the cutest kids?'

'God, so we're talking plural now.'

'Don't worry, I don't want dozens, just two! A boy and a girl to make us the classic nuclear family. You can do the whole stereotypical thing of teaching the boy to play football while I teach our daughter the magic of music.'

'One, it would be rugby if anything, and, two, it could be the other way around, with you teaching her football and me for a change doing something creative with the boy.'

'Hey, look at you getting in touch with your nurturing side. But let's cross that bridge when we come to it. So are you saying you'd like to do this?'

'I say let's do it straight away.'

Evie squealed as I grabbed hold of her and pulled her into me.

FROM THAT MOMENT ON, life just seemed to get better and better, an endless parade of joyous days. Not only were we now trying to conceive a child, but as spring arrived in full force my research in Wytham accelerated. I was also really enjoying lecturing at the university. It turned out that working with the students was something I was naturally good at. And I certainly enjoyed the contrast with my solitary work up in the woods. Although solitary wasn't often the case as Evie accompanied me there regularly to slave away on her fourth movement.

The one person missing from this idyllic period of our lives was Silva. We hadn't see him once in the intervening months. We'd both started to worry that something had happened to him, but when I asked around no one who worked in Wytham had come across our mystery man.

It was summer and we were rapidly approaching the end of the academic year. I'd been marking papers and that had taken longer than I expected. It was beginning to grow dark as I cycled back through Oxford and unusually the streets were almost deserted, a near miracle in our normally bustling city.

I turned on to the home stretch of St John Street and could see the small park in Wellington Square ahead. Our flat at the top of a town house looked out on to this park.

Windows along the street glowed with the lives beyond, while overhead a few cirrus clouds in the clear sky were tinged with gold. I was pushing down on the pedals along the final straight when I heard a growl from behind me.

My skin prickled with goosebumps. I recognised that sound instantly. I glanced back to see the huge black dog from the woods bounding down the street after me.

Shit!

How had that hell hound tracked me down here? The woods was one thing, but here in the city entirely another. Its presence just didn't make sense, but logical or not, the bloody thing was closing in on me.

I leant on the pedals, fighting the heavy dead weight of the mountain bike to accelerate. Despite my efforts, I heard the heavy slap of the beast's paws on the tarmac growing louder.

Cold sweat ran down my back. I lowered myself over my handlebars, pedalling harder, my chest feeling as if it might explode.

I reached the square, tilting the bike over hard as I sped around the bend. Muscles burning, I raced towards the steps of our house that faced the entrance to the park.

If that thing got me, this wasn't going to end well.

As the dog began barking I hopped the bike over the kerb and skidded to a stop. I leapt off, adrenaline pumping though me. I didn't pause and took the steps three at a time as I fumbled in my pocket for my keys.

The dog's barking grew deafening. I shoved the key into the lock, but it wouldn't go in. Then I realised it was upside down.

'Fuck!' I shouted, but there was no one around to hear me.

I braced myself for the snap of jaws on my calves, but then the barking faded away.

Every fibre of my being was trembling as I turned around. My bike was abandoned at the bottom of the stairs but there was no dog to be seen anywhere.

My mind reeled. That just wasn't possible. Something that big couldn't just vanish like that.

I felt my gums tingle as a strong smell of compost filled my nose. A movement in the park caught my eye. The dog? But then I saw a familiar old man watching me from beneath one of the park trees, concern etched around his eyes.

'Silva?' I called out.

The air seemed to blur around him and then he disappeared too.

What the hell?

Had I been dreaming with my eyes open? Or was this something else? A vision, maybe even a warning? After all, every time I'd seen that dog, something awful had happened next.

I spun around as a sense of dread filled me.

Evie...

I shoved my key back into the lock, this time the right way up. I pushed the door open and sprinted up the stairs towards our attic flat.

CHAPTER 9

My latest vision of the black dog was still echoing through me, its touch blurring the line between conscious and unconsciousness thought. Despite finding Evie fine after I'd rushed up to the flat, the experience had left me rattled. The following day I was still trying to figure it out as Evie and I parked our bicycles on the racks outside the John Radcliffe Hospital.

'So what do you say to us beginning a long weekend afterwards to celebrate me being fully signed off?' Evie said.

I'd done everything I could to hide my anxiety from Evie and kept my tone light. 'You sound confident.'

Her face shone with enthusiasm. 'I've never been so sure of anything in my life.'

And maybe Evie was right to be. After all, her results pointed towards a complete remission. That was the logical conclusion. I needed to shake myself out of the mood the vision had left me with and share some of Evie's positivity.

'Maybe we should spoil ourselves and try to catch a West End play for a bargain price?' I said as we headed into the hospital.

'Now you're talking my language. And I'm already ahead of

you. It was going to be a surprise, but since you've just suggested it I've booked this amazing Airbnb apartment in St Pancras Station's clock tower. You're going to love it.'

We were about to enter the outpatients waiting room when Evie tugged at my hand and made me look at her. 'Adam, we have another reason to celebrate today.'

'What do you mean?'

She chewed her lip. 'I didn't want to tell you until I was absolutely sure.'

'Sure of what?'

Evie took my other hand and looked up into my face, scrutinising it for my reaction. 'I missed my period a couple of weeks ago. I did a pregnancy test this morning.'

I stared at her, a fluttery feeling building in my stomach.

She grimaced as I paused. 'I'm so blowing this. I'd planned to whisk you away to London and tell you over a glass of champagne tonight – well, for you at least. But the waiting is killing me, so to hell with that plan.'

My thoughts whirled like leaves in the wind.

I gawped at her. 'Is this really happening?'

Evie gazed into my eyes and it felt as if she was peering directly into my soul. She gave me a nervous smile. 'Yes… I know it's still early days, but still…'

Joy surged through my chest, burning away any lingering shadow left by the vision of the night before. I grabbed hold of Evie and spun her around as I whooped, before lowering her back to the floor.

'You're happy about this then, Adam? I mean, I know we were planning this, but it actually becoming a reality is on a whole other level.'

'Happy, Evie? I'm ecstatic.' I pulled her to me for a kiss before releasing her again. 'I can't wait to see you with your baby.'

'Ours, Adam,' she corrected me.

'Ours…' I could feel myself grinning like a happy drunk guy, but I didn't care. 'God, when can we start telling people?'

'I don't want to jinx it, so maybe let's wait a few weeks before we roll out the news. Perhaps we could get all our friends together to do the big *ta-da* announcement,' she said, fluttering her hands as if she'd just come to the end of her big solo number on stage. 'But I'll need to tell Mum and Dad first.'

'Absolutely. I just wish my folks were still alive. They would have loved this.' I scraped my hand through my hair. 'Jesus, this is all happening so fast. But don't get me wrong. This is fantastic news, Evie.'

She smiled at me. 'Isn't it just?' She drummed her finger on her lips. 'There is absolutely no way I will be able to hide this from Sarah or Matt, though. I mean, keeping it from you was hard enough, but it will be impossible with my sister. She's almost psychic when it comes to me.'

'Then we'll just have to tell them and swear them to silence until we do the big reveal,' I said, as hand in hand we entered the outpatients department.

~

THE MOMENT we entered Dr Reece's office I could tell something was wrong from Sarah's behaviour, who seemed unable to make direct eye contact with us. However, Dr Reece was her usual smiling self as she asked us to sit, even throwing in a bit of small talk about how nice the weather had been. But my attention kept wandering back to Sarah, whose gaze continually slid back to the notes in her lap.

My skin grew clammy as Dr Reece sat forward in her chair, her eyes only for Evie.

'We have just received the results from your blood tests,' she said.

Sarah tipped her head back to stare at the ceiling, pink creeping up her neck towards her ears.

In that instant I knew exactly what Dr Reece was going say, underlined by the look of compassion now on her face.

I clenched my hand, sinking the tips of my nails into my palms as Evie narrowed her eyes.

'Go on…' she said.

Dr Reece's lips thinned. 'I'm afraid we have bad news. Your lymphocyte and white blood cell counts have been heading back upwards again, Evie. It appears that your targeted therapy treatment has failed.'

Failed. It was such a small word, but powerful enough to sweep away the foundations of the new life we'd started to build in an instant.

Sarah lowered her gaze to look directly at Evie, her eyes glittering. 'I'm so sorry.'

But worst of all were the tears now streaming down Evie's face.

To see her crumbling like that broke me more than anything else could have. Suddenly I couldn't breathe and the room started to spin as sobs rose up through me. A moment later it was Evie wrapping her arms around me as convulsions wracked my chest, when it should have been me comforting her.

'It's all right, Adam, we'll get through this somehow,' she said into my ear, lightly kissing the side of my head. She turned back to Dr Reece. 'And there was me so sure I was okay.'

'You had every reason to be. You were making such good progress,' Dr Reece replied gently.

Evie rubbed my back as I attempted to pull myself together. Sarah had already pushed a box of tissues towards me after helping herself to a handful. But far from admonishing the junior doctor, Dr Reece gave Sarah and us the time to compose ourselves. She got it. Everyone in that room got it. This was a tragedy that simply shouldn't have been happening but was. The universe's idea of the worst practical joke.

A strong sense of déjà vu ran through me. I knew then that something had been worried deep within my subconscious, anticipating exactly this moment. Yes, that awful dog vision really had been a premonition, part of my psyche warning me about what we were about to step into.

As Evie dabbed my face with tissues, sorting out my tears like a parent dealing with their child, Sarah took a deep breath and settled herself into her seat before looking at us again.

Here it came. Their plan, or at least what there was of it.

'As we're out of other options, I think we now have to look seriously at a bone marrow transplant,' Sarah said, her expression tight.

A glimmer of hope, a small candle flame seen across a dark ocean – tiny but there.

I reached out for it. 'So what does that entail?' I asked.

'We need to find a suitable donor who's a good match for Evie,' Sarah said. 'But I have to warn you now, Evie, that there is a chance we won't find anyone who fits. And even if we do, it'll be a seriously exhausting course of treatment.'

Evie shrugged. 'I'm so used to that.'

'We know you are,' Dr Reece said.

My brow furrowed. 'Well, if you're looking for a donor, you can start with me.'

Evie looked at me with so much love in her eyes that it made my heart ache.

'I'm afraid it might not be that easy,' Dr Reece said. 'To be a suitable donor the person has to be a close blood match to the patient. We will, of course, run some tests to check your suitability, Adam, but it's unlikely that you'll be suitable as you're not biologically related. It's not impossible, just hugely improbable, so you need to prepare yourself for that eventuality.'

Sarah scraped a loose strand of hair back over her ear. 'But it's a different matter with me. We're going to make it a priority that I get tested straight away to see if my bone marrow is suitable.'

Dr Reece's gaze locked on to us. 'And just to be clear, this is not a small thing that your sister is volunteering for. A bone marrow transplant will leave Sarah weak and she will need time to recover.'

'You'd really do that for me?' Evie asked.

'Do you really need to ask?' Sarah replied.

Evie reached out and took hold of her sister's hand. 'God, I love you so much.'

Sarah nodded, fresh tears trickling from her eyes. 'Me too.'

But then Evie's eyes widened. 'Oh god, what about my baby?'

Sarah and Dr Reece stared at her.

The seconds stretched onwards, an awful moment where nobody seemed to be even breathing until Sarah finally spoke. 'You're pregnant?'

'Only just, but yes,' Evie replied.

Dr Reece's professional mask slipped and she grimaced. 'I'm afraid your foetus is highly unlikely to survive the chemo you'll need to help the transplant take hold.'

Evie's ashen face turned to me. She fell into my arms, clinging on to my back, and began to sob.

CHAPTER 10

Spring daffodils started to appear from the ground the following week, marking the next stage of our emotional roller-coaster ride, with its whiplash plunges and heart-rending twists. The one bright spot was that Sarah had been confirmed as a suitable donor and the bone marrow transplant was already planned. It turned out she only needed a few days off work, although it took another fifteen days for Sarah's own bone marrow levels to return to normal. If she were a car, Sarah would have had two settings: neutral and go fast. She certainly didn't rest properly either, as Matt complained to us both afterwards. She was like a cat pacing the house, according to him, desperate to escape and slowly driving him mad. Eventually he cracked and let her go back to work for the sake of their marriage.

Over the next two months, Evie's journey was very different to that of her sister's. She was left severely weakened as her body fought to boot up its new immune system, and spent the those two months in hospital. Dr Reece put her on an intensive course of total-body irradiation to kill off any remaining cancer cells, draining her energy reserves even further. But, like always, Evie was stoic, even laughing at Matt's awful jokes when he visited her in hospital.

As for me, my days blurred into each other as I spent every moment I could by Evie's side, living every step of the journey with her as much as was humanly possible when you weren't the patient. It was the hardest thing to watch the woman I loved going through what was little short of absolute torture, albeit torture that was our last chance to cure her. If I could have swapped roles with her I would have done so in a heartbeat, anything to take her pain away.

We never talked about the loss of our child. Sarah arranged a controlled abortion rather than allowing the foetus to be subjected to the treatment Evie had to suffer. As though that tragedy wasn't enough, an attempt to harvest her eggs for later down the line had failed. And there was that awful single word again – failed. We would never be able to have children together, not biological ones at least.

Sarah had tried to suggest as gently as she could that we could still adopt one day, but that wasn't a conversation either of us were ready for yet...maybe never.

Evie's hospital room was now our cell, since Dr Reece had told us that Evie couldn't even go outside because of the risk of infection. Even I had to wear a face mask around her. Lilly and James were frequent visitors, as was Matt and a cascade of other friends. But their words often dripped with grief, concern and anger at the universe – a hundred flavours of emotion that you experience when someone you love is fighting for their life.

Meanwhile Evie and I just concentrated on placing one foot in front of the other each and every day. We no longer spoke of the future, as though doing so would jinx it.

The college was fantastic, supporting me in every way possible and giving me as much time off as I needed.

Everyone knew this treatment was almost the last roll of the dice for Evie, although a second bone marrow transplant wasn't out of the question if the first one didn't take. However, Dr Reece had already said she doubted Evie's body would cope with going through the procedure a second time.

So this was almost certainly it, a last Hail Mary to the cosmos, and we all knew it.

Still, finally Evie was allowed home, liberating her from that hospital-room prison. Yes, there was much weighing down on our souls, but there were also occasional brief flurries of laughter in our flat again.

The day after we'd arrived home, Evie asked me to stand before her like a child summoned by a head teacher to their office, although in this instance it was the sofa in front of our TV.

'I have an announcement, Adam,' she began.

I was half expecting her to give me the speech that I'd been dreading, telling me to get on with my life after she'd gone. I definitely didn't expect what came next.

'I'm done with seeing you with a face as long as donkey's moping around here. I know you might not be ready to start teaching again, but at the very least you can get back to your research work up in Wytham.'

'I can't leave you, Evie, not when you've only just been discharged from hospital.'

But she was already prepared with a reply. 'I knew you'd say that, but you needn't worry as I'll be with you. I've spoken to Dr Reece and she said that the chance of infection should be low by now, as long as I'm sensible and don't snog anyone with chickenpox… Okay, my words not hers! I've got to be honest, I'm being selfish here too. I'm ready to finish the final act of my symphony. And before you say that I could do that just as well here, I can't and you know it. Every time I try, the music won't come. But there is something about Wytham that seems to encourage my muse to come out to play. Besides, I always find it energising when I'm up there. That's exactly what I need right now.'

I couldn't really argue with that, and I didn't try. And so the next day, and every day following for the next week, we went up to Wytham Woods.

Spring was well underway as I helped Evie walk through the woods on that seventh day, her leaning on the walking pole that she hated to use but now needed in order to move anywhere. Blue carpets of bluebells covered much of the ground and the birdsong ramped up to rock-concert levels as feathered suitors strutted their stuff for the coming mating season.

Even the sun managed to put in an appearance after a long succession of grey days, although the temperature was only just in double figures. I drove Evie up to the woods in our newly purchased car. It was a necessary luxury with Evie's condition, and had freed of us from relying on taxis.

As had become our daily routine for the last week, Evie sat at the base of Arwen with her back against her trunk. She was wearing a jumper, fleece and woolly hat, and was wrapped in a blanket. She might have looked ready for an Antarctic expedition, but it was the only way I'd allow her in the woods while there was still a chill in the air.

But already I could see for myself that agreeing had been the right call, not that I'd had much choice. Evie's pencil darted this way and that over the blank music sheets as the final movement of her symphony took shape. And, best of all, she looked lit up from the inside by what she was doing. For the first time in months, the Evie I knew had surfaced from the prison cell of her exhaustion to do what she was born to do.

She caught me looking at her. 'What?'

'Nothing, apart from the fact I was thinking just how much I love you.'

'Then that makes two of us.'

Evie blew me a kiss and bent her head back to her work.

I returned my attention to my laptop where I'd just finished linking every variety of tree within a hundred-metre radius. I had used a mesh network to connect the sensors, which I could eventually expand to cover the entire woods as I'd originally planned.

All the live sensors now indicated they had a stable connection with the wireless network and were starting to receive data. One of the computing postgraduates at college had written me a three-dimensional visualiser for the data and this would be my first test run of it. Raw numbers had been my bread and butter throughout my research, but being able to actually see what was going on in real time would be incredible.

I opened up the visualiser and clicked on the connect button. At once individual pixels started to appear and build on the screen, soon beginning to trace routes beneath the ground, picked up by my electrical activity sensors.

'Oh wow, it's actually working,' I said.

'What is?' Evie asked, looking up.

'The visualiser a student wrote for me.' I angled the screen towards her, which now showed a complex series of interconnected lines. I dragged my finger across the pad, rotating the view of the image.

'Wow, that's just a bit pretty. It sort of reminds me of one of my full-body MRI scans, but of the trees and their root systems.'

'Oh, this is more than just the roots. This map also shows the mycorrhizal network connections that the electrical pulses are travelling along.'

'The nervous system of the woods?'

'Exactly.'

Evie leant in towards the screen and pointed. 'What's that knot of light in the middle?'

I zoomed in on where she was indicating. A massive tangle of roots was connected to the broad trunk that the lines of energy appeared to be flowing to and from.

A slow smile filled my face as I read the marker floating over the image next to it. 'That's our very own Arwen.'

Evie turned and gazed at the tree. 'According to your data map, it looks as if she's pretty much at the centre of the action.'

I thought of Silva telling me exactly that at the end of the previous year. How could he have known this stuff? In fact, the more I thought about him – even if I dismissed the vision of him appearing in Wellington Square, which wasn't easy – the more mysterious the guy became.

'I think Arwen being the main hub of the whole woods makes a lot of sense, especially as she's over three hundred and fifty years old. I'm not surprised she's at the centre of things.'

Evie peered into my face. 'Shouldn't you be more excited by this? After all, you've been working towards this for a long time.'

She was right. I was feeling totally flat. I shrugged. 'It's hard to get enthusiastic about anything right now.'

Evie took my hand in hers and started to do her circle-tracing thing on my hands. 'No, you should be enjoying this, Adam. Don't let my bloody cancer steal the happiness out of everything we do. I'm certainly not going to let it get in the way of my music and you should do the same with your trees.'

She held my gaze with her eyes until I eventually nodded. 'My head says you're right, of course, but getting my heart to agree might prove tricky.'

'How about trying the *fake it till you make it* strategy?' Evie replied.

'Maybe I'll try that.'

'Good.' She cupped my face in her hand and kissed me.

As I returned my attention to the screen, I couldn't help wondering if Evie was using her *fake it* strategy now too. She was the world's best actor when she wanted to be. What if she wasn't doing as well as she was pretending? I glanced across at her, but saw only a genuine look of total absorption on her face. No, whatever was going on with her body, this place was definitely good for her. Maybe that was what mattered more than anything right now. I knew I should draw some solace from that.

Over the next hour I began to experiment with the visualiser program, trying out different options, including the ability to colour-code different frequencies of data. When I toggled that on, the tangled web became clear highways of colour, with each tree given its own distinct hue. What was immediately obvious was that the electrical pulses from each type of tree were very distinct. The oaks like Arwen had clear lines of communication between each other, as did a couple of hornbeams on the edge of my mesh sensor network. It appeared that mycorrhizal fungus acted like an agnostic wired network, taking data from everyone and sharing it to their intended target. That would also support the premise that mother trees could send nutrients to other trees of their own type and vice versa via this same system. Although I'd understood the theory for some time, witnessing it like this was quite another thing.

There was an option on the screen to build up an animated view of the woods, although I knew it would take at least ten minutes to capture enough data to work. Compared to human physiology, the wood wide web ran in slow motion. I clicked the icon and waited.

Evie was now humming to herself, every so often frowning and crossing something out on a music sheet before recommencing.

As I looked into the woods, I realised I was keeping a wary eye out for the dog that still haunted my thoughts. I'd mentioned the beast to the conservator at Wytham, who'd later come back to me to say his team had checked the perimeter fence and there were no obvious holes through which the dog could have entered. That ruled out a stray. The most likely explanation was that it had been the dog of some pig-headed member of public, who'd take it upon themselves to ignore the signage and bring their dog in anyway. Maybe the owner had realised their mistake belatedly and hadn't repeated it. I certainly hadn't seen the dog this last week. And as for the demon version of it, I wasn't planning to tell anyone about that ever.

A cascade of notes from Evie's Chinese flute flurried around her as she began to play. This was new – Evie's first airing of her symphony's final movement. The breath caught in my throat from almost the first moment the vibrations hit my eardrums. This music was so Evie, and to listen to it was like listening to her soul reverberating the universe around her.

I listened, transfixed by the perfect spell as the melody grew in intensity, spreading out into the woods in rolling waves of pure emotion. The notes seemed to weave around the birdsong, just like the first time I'd heard them, or they began to weave their song around it – I couldn't be sure. The only thing that I could be certain of was this was one of those songs that would touch the hearts of all who heard it. Maybe in its own small way the echo of it would make the world a slightly better place. What I was listening to was, without doubt, a work of genius.

The real world came rushing back in as a loud repeated beeping sound came from my laptop. I immediately hit mute but the spell had been broken and Evie was lowering her flute.

'Sorry, I didn't mean to interrupt you!' I told her. 'Please carry on.'

'No, I actually found that a bit knackering. But what did you think?'

'Think? Oh, Evie, it's spectacular, breathtaking and every other incredible adjective in the English language.'

She tapped her pencil on the sheet of music in time to an inaudible rhythm. 'You really think so?'

I leant over and grasped her hands in mine. 'I know so. Does this mean that it's finished?'

'Almost. Just few minor tweaks and I'll be happy with it. Oh, and I need to come up with a name for it. After all, if I die, "Unfinished Symphony" has already been taken quite a few times over.' The corners of her mouth curled up.

But that was too close to home for me and I couldn't manage a smile in return.

Evie's face fell. 'Sorry, Adam, ignore me and my gallows humour. Anyway, why was your laptop making that awful racket? Has it crashed or something?'

'No idea.' I turned to look at the screen.

A message was flashing on it: *Electrical surge detected.* I peered at the words, confused.

'Is something wrong?' Evie asked.

'Not exactly wrong, but maybe something very interesting just happened. Hang on and let me find out.' I cancelled the message and looked at the visualiser window. The mother tree was shining like a million-watt light bulb. 'What the hell?'

'Don't keep me in a suspense here,' Evie said, craning her neck to look at the screen.

I peered at the data coming in. 'It seems as if our mother tree got a bit shouty just now and sent a massive electrical surge out through the mycorrhizal network.'

Evie turned around and patted the trunk with her hand. 'Sorry, old girl, did I wake you up with my music?'

I stared at her and then the tree. Then I quickly pulled up the replay icon and wound back a couple of minutes. I pressed play and watched the timestamp on the simulation. The tree started to glow around its base where Evie had been sitting.

'My god, Evie, play again.'

'Hey, I was only joking.'

'You may have been, but I'm not. It seems Arwen lit up like a Christmas tree when you started to play.'

Evie tilted her head to look at me. 'You're being serious?'

'Absolutely, but to be sure, let's try once more.'

'Okay…'

Evie raised the flute back to her lips and began to play.

I toggled the visualiser to a real-time display and the effect was instantaneous. Cascades of light were pulsing in the trunk of the ancient oak in time to her music. But, more than that, in the simulation I could see this light spreading through the mycorrhizal network and lighting up every tree connected to it.

'Oh my god, Evie, you haven't just woken up Arwen, but the whole flipping woods!'

Evie lowered her flute and stared at me. 'But surely that's impossible. I mean, it's not as if the trees have ears or anything.'

'Maybe not, but all sounds are basically vibrations travelling through the air, vibrations that could be picked up by a tree's leaves, branches, even picked up by the roots through the ground.'

'Okay, but even if that's true, sound vibrations must hit trees all the time, so why would my music have such a dramatic effect? I mean, I've heard of people talking to plants to help make them grow, but this...'

The implications started to hit me. 'My god, Evie. If this is true, trees responding to music is going to be a whole area of research in itself. It could even point towards a rudimentary consciousness. And I wouldn't have discovered the language of the Ents without you. They must have great taste in music.'

Evie laughed and pulled me into a tight hug before suddenly pulling away again. 'And will you look who has just turned up. Hello, stranger.'

Silva was heading towards us, a wide smile on his face. 'Was it you playing that celestial music of the angels, Evie?'

She nodded and even found the energy to stand up and head towards Silva to embrace him. 'So what you been up to for all these months?'

'Here, there and everywhere.' His hand reached out for mine and shook it. 'And how are you doing, Adam?'

I caught the hint of a larger question in his tone and I peered at him for a moment too long. 'Better now...'

He slowly nodded as if we'd had a far bigger conversation than these few exchanged words would suggest.

'That's good to hear,' he said. He turned to Evie. 'And how about you?'

She pulled a face. 'There's a lot to tell.'

'I can imagine. But I've got plenty of time to hear it if you have the time.' His eyes strayed to the plastic boxes containing our picnic.

'Oh, we have,' Evie said, setting down her flute.

I wished I could ask him if he'd really been in Wellington Square that night the phantom dog had tracked me down in Oxford. But there was no way I could do that without sounding completely crazy.

So we shared our food with Silva and began to tell him everything that had happened since we'd last seen him.

CHAPTER 11

Over the next few months, as summer took hold, we visited Wytham Woods as frequently as we could.

'My music practically writes itself among these trees,' Evie once said to me.

And it didn't just seem to be her artistic work that was flourishing up here either as Evie had put the final touches to her already very polished, to my ear at least, symphony. The results of her bone marrow transplant had been very promising. Unfortunately, a real crisis with one of my students who'd insisted that it was only me who could persuade them from dropping out of the course, had meant that I hadn't been able to make the consult. So Evie had gone by herself and had told me that Dr Reece had confirmed that her immune system was now nicely rebooting. Even though Evie's energy levels were still through the floor, everything now pointed to her making a full recovery. It seemed our Hail Mary to the cosmos had been listened to by someone.

However, Evie also credited her time in the woods as playing a big part. I could see this with my own eyes. Often she would arrive in the woods absolutely exhausted, but by the time we left

Evie would be a new woman who could increasingly walk without any assistance.

Day by day, week by week, I felt a weight lifting off my shoulders. And for maybe the first time I allowed myself to get really excited about my research work.

The data was showing a very direct correlation between Evie's music and a physiological reaction to it from the trees. Through further experiments we'd found that other music also caused an electrical spike in activity, with one exception – heavy metal, which if anything had a dampening effect on the trees' electrical activity. We'd even discovered that reading poems and extracts from books registered a reaction, especially in Arwen.

My research work had taken on a life of its own and, despite swearing a few colleagues at work to secrecy until I was ready to publish, the inevitable happened. Rumours began to swirl through the corridors of the Oxford colleges like a summer storm wind. Before long it became an open secret to the point that my students started to volunteer their help with a project they weren't even meant to know about. In addition, a succession of sponsors stepped forward, offering to fully fund my work. I suddenly found myself with more money available for pursuing my ideas than I knew what to do with.

Evie and I often talked about creative ways to spend the money. The front runner was Evie's idea of heading to the Amazon rainforest to carry on my research there – when she had fully recovered.

In the meantime, Wytham became our whole world, a place where the dreams of both of us were nurtured and flourished. Then there was Silva, our very own wise old man of the woods, now a regular fixture of our days here, often dropping by to see how we were getting on. Our friendship quickly developed and he left me astonished at his knowledge of all things flora and fauna more than once. The guy was a walking Wikipedia and he seemed very intrigued but not surprised by what my research had revealed.

It was another typical summer's day at Wytham. The lazy warmth of the building morning heat wrapped around us, the air almost thick on our limbs as we headed into the woods.

Evie spread out today's feast on brightly coloured plastic picnic plates with floral patterns. A series of plastic boxes contained a selection of bite-sized soft tacos. She'd prepared them the previous night with various fillings, from roasted sweet potato with coriander and feta to a sensational crab and lime creation.

I helped myself to my sixth taco. 'Evie, I can't stop eating these and I blame you. They are far too good.'

She smiled at me. 'Well, thank you. I love the recipes from that fusion cookbook you bought me for my birthday.'

'As presents go, it has to be my best investment ever.'

She raised her eyebrows at me. 'Yes, cunning, very cunning, Adam. It's certainly been fun experimenting with my cooking. I've been seriously thinking about getting into baking next.'

'You'll be on one of those TV bake-off programmes before long.'

Evie laughed, something that she was doing a lot more of these days. Then she raised her chin towards something over my shoulder. 'I swear that man has the nose of bloodhound. It's as if he can smell food from right across the woods.'

I turned and wasn't surprised to see Silva heading towards us.

'Hello, my friends,' he said, his eyes already zeroing in on the boxes of tacos on the picnic blanket. 'My goodness, those look rather appetising.'

'Go on, help yourself,' Evie said. 'I know you want to.'

Silva chuckled. 'Am I that transparent?'

'Absolutely,' I replied with a smile.

'Ah, then I'm guilty as charged,' he replied.

As Evie put together a selection of tacos on a plate for him, Silva lowered himself on to a fallen bough and laid out a blue handkerchief on his lap, a tradition when he ate with us.

Silva always made a show of enjoying her food and this time was no exception. He picked up one of the crab tacos and closed his eyes as he wafted it under his nose. 'This smells like Irish sea mist that's just rolled in to cover the leaves of the trees that border the English Channel.'

I raised my eyebrows at Evie and she grinned.

Silva opened his mouth wide. With a flourish of his hand, he placed the crab taco into his mouth and began to chew.

'So what do you think?' Evie asked.

Silva held up a finger to silence her and continued to chew. Then he swallowed and let out a long sigh as his eyes snapped open. 'It tastes like angels have just danced a tango across my taste buds. You, Evie, are just as gifted with conjuring up culinary delights as you are with music.'

She beamed at him. 'Oh, you old charmer.'

His gaze turned to my laptop as he helped himself to another taco. 'So how are things going with your research work today, Adam?'

'Really well, actually,' I said. 'My students finished placing the rest of the mesh sensor network throughout the woods at the weekend. Although I need to complete calibrating the sensors, the first data has started to roll in and it's pretty spectacular. Would you like to see it?'

'I most certainly would,' Silva replied.

A moment later I had the visualiser open with a zoomed-out aerial view of the whole of Wytham Woods. On it was displayed the vast mycorrhizal network in all its multicoloured splendour. Individual trees sat in the centre of their own gossamer cobwebs of pulsing light, all linked to each other by millions of connections.

Evie looked over my shoulder. 'I still can't believe just how beautiful it is.'

'For those who've never seen it before it will no doubt take their breath away,' Silva said, as if this didn't include him and wasn't anything exceptional.

Like always, I was struck by his lack of reaction. He was fascinated with what I was doing, but nothing I showed him seemed to surprise him.

Evie pulled a face at me behind his back. 'You should tell Silva about your news, Adam.'

His eyes sharpened as he turned to me. 'What news is that?'

'Just the realisation of a lifelong dream. I've been asked to do a TED Talk about my work here in Wytham.'

Silva scratched his beard. 'A TED Talk?'

Evie's expression widened. 'You must have heard of them?'

He gave her a blank look. 'No, I can't say I have.'

She flapped a hand at me. 'Then over to you, Adam, to explain it.'

'A TED event is where people give talks that everyone can watch around the world on the internet. They cover everything, including the arts and the sciences. From the power of rejection to how bees are disappearing from our world and need to be protected.'

Evie nodded. 'And to be asked to give a TED Talk is a very big deal, Silva.'

I smiled at her. 'I've always dreamt of giving one, but never really imagined I would ever get the chance.'

'Oh, I see. It certainly sounds like something very important,' Silva said.

'It really is,' Evie replied. 'But I still can't believe you haven't heard about them before. When you get home you should look up some on the internet.'

Silva pulled a face at her. 'I've never bothered with anything like that. I never will. I've seen far too many people wandering through these woods spending their time looking at the small computers in their hands rather than at the wonders of the world around them.'

I peered at him and then realised what he meant. 'Oh, you mean phones. Yes, you may have a point there.'

Evie nodded. 'I know exactly what you mean. People tune out and always look for distractions. They don't tune in. That's one of the reasons I love making music. When I'm composing, it sometimes feels as if I'm listening to the heartbeat of the universe.'

Silva smiled. 'Now that I really do understand.'

'Hey, not all computers are bad,' I said. 'Mine is absolutely essential to my work. Without it, I'd never be able to see the mycorrhizal network in all its glory – and to share that with others. What we're revealing here will have a profound effect on our understanding of how woodlands function and may even help to change some of the hardened attitudes to things like global warming. A lot of eyes are being opened by what we're discovering.'

'It's about time,' Silva replied.

'What do you mean?' Evie asked.

'I mean, this is something people used to know, but seem to have forgotten in your modern world. The knowledge has sadly been lost.'

I couldn't help but notice his use of *your*. Obviously, Silva was old school, someone whom the twenty-first century had left far behind. But he seemed entirely comfortable with that arrangement. He probably didn't even own a microwave. Yet what he was saying was also deeply intriguing.

'Can you give me an example about this lost knowledge?' I asked.

'Where do you think all your folklore about woods and trees comes from? For centuries people saw woods and trees as something magical, but this understanding fell away in recent times.

Can you imagine what it was like when Albion was covered with woods just like this remnant here at Wytham?'

'Albion?' Evie asked.

'The ancient name for this land,' Silva replied. 'It was a truly magical time, when this realm was watched over by an army of mother trees. Imagine what your mycorrhizal network would have looked like then...' Silva had a faraway gaze in his eyes as he spoke.

I stared at the guy. He was starting to sound as if he was in the fifteenth century not the twenty-first.

'You know, you really are a poet when you talk like this,' Evie said. 'If you wrote these things down, I'm sure a lot of people would love to read them.'

Silva shook his head. 'I've always been one for the oral tradition of storytelling. Let the scholars capture their thoughts in dusty books to be forgotten on the shelves of countless libraries.' He frowned and looked into the distance.

I caught Evie's eye and she shrugged.

It wasn't the first time Silva had gone off on one of his verbal rambles, but it wasn't hard to pick up on the underlying sadness in his tone. But then again I supposed that was what so many older people did: think back with rose-tinted glasses to a time when life was so much better than it could ever be now. I'd once heard a psychologist refer to it as selective amnesia. But who were we to challenge an old man's memories of an older, better world where ambrosia flowed through rivers and every day was a perfect summer's day?

Silva's expression brightened then and his gaze fell on Evie like a landing butterfly. 'And how is your magnificent symphony coming along, my dear?'

'Another week and I think it'll be finished,' she replied.

He clapped his hands together. 'Oh, that's the most wonderful news.'

'And the trees obviously adore what she's written so far,' I said.

'You should see how they light up when she plays – and not just in the immediate vicinity. Arwen seems to send electrical impulses out to the entire woods whenever Evie is performing.'

Evie grinned. 'It's as if our mother tree is the DJ playing my music on Wytham Woods Radio for the other trees to enjoy.'

Silva smiled. 'Of course she does. Your music, Evie, is something truly wonderful for the trees.'

She laughed. 'If you say so.'

'I do.' His eyes narrowed her on her. 'And how are you doing in yourself?'

He knew by now that Evie was having treatment for acute leukaemia, although when we'd told him it was almost as if he already knew.

Her gaze fell away from his. 'I'm doing really well.'

Silva opened his mouth and closed it again, as if he'd thought better of what he was about to say.

Evie chewed her lip as she held up one of her plastic boxes. 'Anyway, you must try one of these chilli tomato tacos, although I'd better warn you they will blow your head off.'

Silva's eyes held hers for a moment, but then he nodded as he took one. 'Oh, I can handle quite a bit of chilli.'

Evie quickly turned away and busied herself tidying up our plates.

I looked between them with the distinct impression they'd just had a conversation without any words – a conversation I'd been deliberately left out of. A sense of unease filled me as I made a mental note to tackle Evie about it later.

~

SILVA HAD FINALLY LEFT us and melted away into the woods. Now we were alone again, and as the leaves murmured around us a deep sense of stillness settled in the woods. There wasn't even a bird to be heard.

Evie had been resting her head against Arwen's trunk as she scribbled notations on her music sheets.

I hadn't been able to shake my growing sense of unease that she was holding something back from me and it was near impossible to concentrate on my work. The numbers on the screen might as well have been written in hieroglyphics.

I took a mental deep breath. I needed to talk to Evie and I needed to do it now.

At that precise moment I heard the barest whisper on the gentle breeze.

'Adam…' Evie's voice said.

I turned around to look at her but she was fast asleep. I licked my suddenly dry lips.

'Adam…' the voice came again.

But this time I was certain it wasn't Evie. Her mouth remained closed, her chest gently rising and falling. Somebody had to be playing a prank on me – maybe one of my students.

'Hey, who's there?' I called out into the woods.

Right then the woods felt unreal, as if I'd stepped into the magical version Silva had mentioned.

'Adam, it's all going to be all right,' the phantom voice whispered.

I felt a shimmer of static wash over my skin, raising the hairs on my arms. Then the musical notes of Evie's symphony began to play, so faint it was right at the edge of my hearing. But it had to be coming from somewhere.

I stood up and headed into the woods, trying to follow the sound, but the more I hunted for the source, the more it seemed to be coming from everywhere and nowhere.

What the hell was going on?

A shrill warbling alarm cut through the air. My laptop. I ran back to where I'd left Evie by Arwen.

She was still asleep despite the harsh sound. I rushed to my computer and stared at the screen.

The words *Electrical surge detected* were flashing up on the screen.

Was this linked to the ghostly voice and music I'd heard?

My mouth became bone dry as I opened up the visualiser window.

The air caught in my throat.

On the screen light was pulsing through the entire woods. But there was one key difference to the previous electrical activity surges. Rather than travelling out from Arwen, the exact opposite was happening now. Light was cascading from every tree in Wytham Woods into the ancient oak I was standing next to.

I buried my hands into my hair as I peered at the screen, trying to make sense of what I was seeing. I zoomed in on Arwen, locked my hands around the back of my neck and took a sharp intake of breath.

I stared at the filigree of fine lines knotted at the base of the oak. My pulse amped. It couldn't be. I reoriented the view to match where I was standing in relation to Arwen. And then I knew, I really knew. The knot of light, the target of the energy pouring from the woods, was Evie as she lay asleep at the base of the oak. Her body exactly matched the position of the intense electrical activity that was being detected.

My mind whirled as I tried to figure this out. It looked as if Evie had become part of the mycorrhizal network.

I stared at her and then at the screen in wonder.

Then the summer heat suddenly fell away and my breath was clouding the air.

My stomach tightened into a stone as a shudder passed through the leaves. The music faded away and in the distance I heard it. A new sound. A dog barking. Evie moaned in her sleep and swatted away something with her hands.

I rushed to Evie and cradled her in my arms as the chilled air began to evaporate and the summer warmth rushed back in.

Her eyes flickered open and she stared at me. She began shivering despite the increase in temperature. 'Adam, you're going to need to take me straight to the hospital.'

I felt dizzy as the hundred thoughts about what I'd just witnessed were swept away by sudden and utter fear. 'What's wrong?'

Evie's glistening eyes locked on to mine. 'I'm not doing so well. The truth is, I haven't been for some time.'

I stared at her. 'What you mean?'

'Let's go and see Dr Reece and she'll explain everything,' Evie said as tears began to trickle down her face.

CHAPTER 12

Even with Dr Reece's unearthly powers of professionalism, this time she couldn't disguise the deep furrow in her brow. Meanwhile, Sarah watched both of us with an ashen face. Evie didn't say anything during the drive here; she'd barely looked at me. Now her gaze was steadfastly locked on to Dr Reece.

The doctor leant forward in her chair. 'I'm afraid it's as we suspected, Evie. We've just had your results back from your test last week and your leukaemia is progressing rapidly again since the bone marrow transplant failed. As we've already discussed with you, any further treatment would at best only give you a short reprieve, and would come at considerable cost to yourself. Have you decided what you'd like to do?'

'What do you mean "already discussed with you"?' I stared between them.

Still without looking at me, Evie reached over and gripped my hand. 'I can't face any more chemo, Dr Reece. I just want to make the most of my final months.'

I gawped at her. 'Final months? What are you talking about?'

Sarah blinked rapidly but remained mute.

Evie glanced at me for a brief second before returning her gaze to Dr Reece. 'I'll explain everything.'

Sarah swallowed hard, on the verge of tears as she referred to her notes. 'In that case you'll need to think about the palliative options. As you get weaker you may want to consider coming into hospital for the final period.'

'Final period?' I said. I had to be hearing things. Any second now they would all turn around and shout, 'Gotcha!'

'With all due respect to you guys, I'm not coming back in here ever again if I have any choice in the matter,' Evie replied, looking at me with guilt in her eyes.

Sarah was doing her best not to catch my eye. 'We understand. In which case we could try to secure you a place at the local hospice. The team there are fantastic.'

My heart began to thump in my chest. They couldn't really be saying what I thought they were, could they?

Evie's expression pinched. 'I'm sure they are, but there is only one place I want to be and that's at home for these last few months, or however long I have left.'

I felt a chasm opening up inside me. 'But you told me you were heading towards remission, Evie?'

She turned to me, reached out and took both my hands in hers. 'I'm so sorry, Adam. In my head, I was going to tell you the truth over an expensive bottle of wine that we would share under Arwen's leaves. But I think I've missed that moment. I just hope you can find it in your heart to forgive me. I've been deliberately keeping you in the dark for the last few weeks...' She dropped her gaze to the floor.

I had trouble squeezing the words out of my throat. 'Go on.'

Evie wrung her hands together. 'A month ago they picked up a huge flare in my lymphocyte and white blood cell counts.'

'But you told me that the check-up went fine?'

'I lied to you,' Evie replied flatly, not looking at me again.

I caught Sarah grimacing at Dr Reece.

'You both knew?'

They nodded.

I stared at them. 'Dr Reece I can understand, but, Sarah, how couldn't you tell me?'

'As much as I love you, Adam, I'm committed to patient–doctor confidentiality.'

A stone grew in my gut. 'Well, thanks for bloody nothing.'

Evie looked up at me. 'Hey, don't have a go at Sarah. I swore her and Dr Reece to secrecy.'

I stared at Evie. 'You're really going to die?'

'Hey, we all are, right? It's just that my sell-by date is a lot sooner than yours.'

Her attempt at humour smashed into the hard thing growing inside me, shattering it into pieces. 'How could you keep this from me, Evie?'

Tears pooled in the corners of her eyes. 'Adam, I'm so sorry. I was trying to protect you and give you as much time as possible without the knowledge of this wrecking your happiness.'

'How could you?' I repeated, shooting to my feet, the chair screeching over the worn lino floor. 'I've got to get out of here.'

'Adam, please don't go,' Evie said.

Tears running down her face, she reached for my arm, but I brushed her off.

Sarah opened her mouth but Dr Reece shook her head and she closed it again.

I felt their eyes burning on my back as I turned away. I rushed to the door, throwing it open and slamming it hard behind me. At once, all the eyes in the waiting area were on me.

'Oh, you can all get stuffed too!' I shouted.

I rushed past them, my tears blurring the hospital corridors as I started to run. I had to get away from all of this. I had to get to the only place that made any sense in all this madness.

IN THE DRIZZLE of summer rain, I sat under the mother tree, the feel of its bark pressing into my back. Something inside me had broken and uncontrollable wracking sobs shook me to my core.

Evie, my beautiful Evie, was going to die and leave me utterly alone.

A soft rustling sound came from close by and a tiny wood mouse appeared from the leaf litter like a diver surfacing in an ocean. It pulled itself up on to one of Arwen's exposed roots and ran along it until it was directly opposite me, less than a metre away. It sat up and looked straight at me with not a hint of fear in its eyes. Something about the touch of its gaze quietened the grief inside me and my tears slowed as I took in a shuddering breath.

The mouse bobbed its head a fraction, as if it was nodding to say its work was done, and it scampered away along the root and into a nearby thicket of nettles.

'Are you okay?' Silva's voice said from nearby.

I almost jumped as I turned to see the old man sitting on his fallen bough, looking at me under his bushy eyebrows. I hadn't even heard him approaching.

All I could manage to do was shake my head.

'It's about Evie, isn't it?' he asked.

I found a faint voice and managed to reply. 'She's dying.'

'I already knew,' Silva replied, his tone sympathetic.

My gaze snapped to him. 'What, she told you too?'

Silva shook his head. 'No, but I've been around long enough to have developed an instinct for these sort of things. Am I to gather that she's only just revealed this to you?'

I nodded. 'Evie's known for over a bloody month and deliberately kept it from me.'

'I see…' Silva scratched his beard before he spoke again, his dark eyes glinting with pinpricks of starlight. 'Adam, please listen to me carefully, as this might help you.'

'As though any words can help this.'

'Well, let me try…' He picked up a dead leaf and turned it over in his hand as he contemplated it. 'Think about all the magical moments that you and Evie have shared together and what you've both achieved up here. The symphony that Evie has composed is the rarest of gifts, music that will for ever change people privileged enough to hear it. And you, Adam, a scientist pushing at the boundaries of what is known about trees.' His voice deepened, taking on a sing-song tone. 'Through your work you're revealing how trees are interlinked by a million connections. Maybe that knowledge will even open up some people's eyes to the lie that many of them have come to believe: that humans are separate from the natural world around them, its master rather than its servant. It's a lie reinforced by the way people wall themselves off in the modern world with countless distractions, blinding themselves to the true nature of life. Adam, the truth you have discovered in these woods will have a profound impact on so many people. One day, but not today, when the hole torn out of you by the loss of Evie is filled with fresh hope, you will look back at this time and realise you created something truly wonderful together in these precious months. And what a gift to the world that is.'

His words slipped through the cracks in my grief and somehow found the core of my being. I blinked, like a person waking up, and peered at the tiny stars still flickering in his eyes. 'I would love that to be true, Silva, but this is going to destroy me.'

The old man sighed and nodded. 'To start with, it most certainly will. It will be the storm that shatters everything. But as the storm slowly passes you will begin to remember who you truly are and discover that some connections survive even death.'

'What do you mean?'

'This is a lesson you will need to learn for yourself. Words alone, however well crafted, won't be your own truth until you live them.'

'You do know you're talking in riddles?'

'Yes, an old habit of mine...'

I shook my head. 'But the thing is, Silva, Evie should have told me the moment she found out. It breaks my heart that she's been carrying this around when she should have shared it with me.'

'Evie did it only out of love, Adam. You must see this?'

Just for a second it felt as if the storm clouds had swirled away as a shaft of sunlight blazed down on us. For the first time Silva's words made me think about the reasons behind Evie's lies.

Silva peered into my eyes, into me. 'Evie tried to create a bubble to protect you both. Dealing with her own grief must have taken all her strength.'

This was the truth and the rest was just shadows in my mind. I slowly nodded. 'God, what have I done, Silva? I tore into her when she told me at the hospital.'

'That was just your grief doing the talking, not you, Adam. In my experience, when hurt takes over a person's mouth, it has a knack of choosing exactly the wrong way to express itself.'

'So what should I be saying?'

'That you love Evie, of course!'

I gazed at this wise man of the woods and felt my shoulders drop. 'I've got to go back and apologise, haven't I?'

'Yes, but I promise you it will be okay, Adam. Part of loving is forgiving someone when they have been a complete and utter prat.'

Impossibly, considering the heartache ripping me apart, I found myself smiling.

Silva ran his thumb over the dead leaf in his hand. 'One last word of advice before you leave, Adam. Don't spend your final months together grieving about what you're going to lose. Life is such a precious gift and, as much as you are able to, get on and live it. Build wonderful memories together in the time that you have left. It will be those memories that will one day heal your soul.'

Silva stood up and so did I. He held out his arms and enveloped me in a hug, tapping my back with his palms.

A smell of leaves, wild roses and blackberries filled my

nostrils. The old man's scent was like a concentrated version of the woods itself.

As I turned away, determined to make things right with Evie, I noticed the tiny wood mouse had reappeared and it dipped its head as I passed.

'Did you see that, Silva?' I said.

But there was no reply. When I turned around he'd vanished. The mouse too was gone. Alone again and shaking my head, I set off for home. Impossibly, the weight that had pressed my shoes into the mud felt slightly lighter now than when I'd first entered the woods.

CHAPTER 13

Silva's words to seize each and every day left a lasting impression on me. That was why, despite the deep sense of grief dragging at my heels, I was sitting with Evie two weeks later in the glorious wood-panelled splendour of the drawing room of the Randolph Hotel. Like most people who lived in Oxford, we'd caught glimpses of this esteemed place through the windows as we'd passed by on the pavement. Together with the fact that many memorable episodes of *Inspector Morse,* Oxford's most famous detective, had been filmed here, meant that we'd promised to eventually treat ourselves to high tea here one day. And today was that day.

On the table between us sat a three-tiered silver platter with a selection of delicacies, which had been presented by an old-school waiter wearing a formal black tailed jacket. We'd worked our way first through the sandwiches, the crusts of course removed, then proceeded on to the scones, which had created quite a heated discussion about the right order for the jam and the cream. Now we were on the petits fours.

Evie took a bite out of something that looked like a mini crème brûlée tartlet and a look of complete bliss filled her face.

'Now that is something else. The pastry is so light and the cinnamon custard is just perfect.'

'I'm not sure where you're getting the space to eat any more. I'm already well and truly stuffed.'

'Hey, I can't let these go to waste – they are far too good for the food bin.'

'I'm sure we could ask them for a doggy bag.'

She raised an eyebrow. 'Do you think the Randolph would lower itself to such a thing?'

I smiled. 'I'm sure they'd bend over backwards to keep their patrons happy.' I picked up my porcelain teacup of Darjeeling tea. 'I'd like to propose a toast.'

Smiling, Evie raised up her own cup, her little finger extended. 'To us, my dear,' she said in a suitably posh Oxford accent. 'This is quite the exquisite experience, darling.'

I tried to keep the grin off my face as a passing waiter, raised his eyebrow a fraction at us.

'I'm not sure that he entirely approves of us being here,' I said once he was out of earshot.

'Well, I know where they can stuff that opinion,' Evie said.

'I'll drink to that.' We clinked our cups together.

Evie took out her notebook and crossed off an item on the list. 'Seven days in and five things marked off my bucket list. We're on a roll, Adam.'

It had been me who'd come up with the bucket list idea, a way for Evie to squeeze every last drop of joy from the time still left to her. Unfortunately, her condition meant she was too weak for any serious travel. So seeing Victoria Falls from a helicopter and taking a drive along Route 66 had to be scrubbed. Instead, we'd brainstormed things we could do closer to home – from Evie's one-on-one class with a skilled chocolatier that had resulted in us eating our body weight in exotic chocolate to a trip in a hot-air balloon over Oxford's dreaming spires. Every experience had built on the other like brushstrokes to create a glorious painting of memories.

'So what do you fancy doing next from your list?' I asked.

Evie held up a finger as she finished eating a mini cherry cheesecake, before wiping her mouth with a napkin. 'Wow, so good. Anyway, what to do next…' She scrunched up her eyes as she tapped her plate with a fingertip. 'Well, I've always wanted the excuse to get a posh frock for one of the fancy college balls.'

'Then let's make it happen. I know there's a fundraising ball coming up at Christ Church. I heard the tickets are almost impossible to get your hands on, but I'll do my best to secure us a couple.'

'Don't forget to use the old line about your girlfriend being about to die.'

I couldn't help but flinch.

Evie thinned her lips. 'Sorry, Adam. My gallows humour isn't ever that far away these days.'

'It's okay,' I said, even though I hated the reminder.

This was just a manifestation of the dichotomy of our situation. I might have been all bright smiles and dream-granter on the surface, but on the inside I was barely holding it together. I felt the shadow of *that* day growing ever nearer, only highlighted as the colour slowly faded from Evie's face day by day, a constant reminder of what was to come. Of course, Evie being Evie, she was incredibly pragmatic about everything and would often joke about it. I just wished I could toggle some switch in my mind to be more like her.

She leant across the table and took my hand in hers, giving me a questioning look. 'Actually, there's a secret item on my bucket list that I haven't written down. Can I tell you what it is?'

'As long as it's not the parachute jump you tried to get me to agree to.'

'Nothing like that.' Evie began to draw a circle on the back of my hand. 'Adam, I was wondering if…'

'No wingsuit jumps either.'

Evie laughed. 'Nothing like that.' She took a deep breath. 'Adam, would you please make me the happiest woman on this planet by agreeing to marry me?'

I stared at her, my mind in a state of shock. I certainly hadn't seen that coming. My thoughts scattered like kicked-up autumn leaves, as my heartbeat started to accelerate.

Evie chewed her lip as she watched my internal chaos play out on my face. 'Look, there is absolutely no pressure. You really can say no.'

Then everything came into sharp crystalline focus. This beautiful woman wanted to marry me and maybe create the most magical memory of all. In that moment I'd never wanted anything so much in my life.

I grabbed hold of Evie's hand and pulled her across the table towards me, tipping the tiered silver platter and sending its contents crashing to the floor. I caught the waiter and the other diners watching us in horror. But I ignored all of them as I kissed Evie firmly on the mouth.

She wrapped her arms around me, smiling beneath the kiss. We finally pulled away from each other as the waiter swept towards us.

I turned to him and the other diners, knowing a goofy expression was well and truly on my face. 'She just asked me to marry her,' I threw out there as an explanation.

'And?' an old American guy sitting with his male partner at the next table asked.

'God, yes!' I said to Evie, holding both her hands in mine. 'Yes, a thousand times over.'

Evie threw her arms around me as the dining room, and even the waiter, exploded into spontaneous applause.

CHAPTER 14

It was remarkable what could be achieved when life didn't give you much time. From agreeing a wedding date to gaining permission from Oxford University to hold the ceremony in Wytham Woods and a hundred other things that had to be organised, somehow we achieved the impossible and pulled it off.

On our wedding day, we stood in the growing dusk beneath Arwen with our humanist celebrant Jane. What had to be at least a hundred tea-light jam jars hung from the branches of the oak. Around us a hundred of our closest friends and family sat in deckchairs that had been decorated with creepers of ivy and honeysuckle, which Sarah, our maid of honour, had organised. And everyone had risen to the challenge of the theme, which Evie had chosen: a mash-up of steampunk and *A Midsummer's Night Dream*. The men wore a variety of bowler and top hats, most with goggles strapped to them. Many donned Victorian-style clothing with a few sets of horns thrown in to honour the Shakespeare play. The women had used the theme as an excuse to go wild, from billowy long dresses to steampunk fairies and everything in between. The sum effect of all this planning was that everyone looked spectacular under the candlelight. Evie's objective had been well and truly achieved – to create a quirky wedding with a magical atmosphere that everyone would always remember.

Around us in the woods, trestle tables had been covered with lace tablecloths. The candelabra on each illuminated a riot of food that had been prepared, from Evie's now famous tacos to luxurious handmade pies and puddings that sparkled with edible gold glitter. Beyond the banquet was a full-blown bar where two guys were ready with jam-jar cocktails.

The one person missing was Silva. The mysterious old man had melted away into the woods once again and we hadn't seen him for weeks. Something told me he didn't like crowds, although I was certain he would have loved the banquet.

A group of Evie's musical friends had formed a quartet for the night. I'd hoped she'd use it as an excuse to play her still unnamed symphony, but she'd fobbed me off when I asked, saying she still needed to make a few final tweaks before it was ready for general consumption. So instead the quartet were playing Satie's Gymnopédies, Evie's choice, which turned out to be absolutely perfect.

'This wedding will be the stuff of dreams,' Evie had said. And it already was.

Despite that, it was hard to ignore that everybody around us was crying. It seemed that the poignant nature of this union between us wasn't lost on anyone. I'd spotted Sarah having to redo her eye make-up at least three times already, and Matt's face was bright red from crying when he thought no one could see him.

James and Lilly were stoic, but their grief wasn't far beneath the surface, barely hidden behind a mask of outward cheerfulness. People had floated around them, clearly not sure whether to congratulate them on the coming marriage or console with them on the inevitable loss of their daughter. Everyone gathered there realised that the hardest thing for any parent to face was outliving their child.

And at the centre of the storm of emotion stood Evie and me. I was wearing a red Victorian cavalry outfit, resplendent with gold buttons and a hat with a big white feather on top. Evie had drawn the line at the curved sword, saying it would just get in the way.

But it was Evie herself who really stole the show. Before me she was a woodland fairy come to life. Her dress of blood-red silk, partly transparent to give it an ethereal feel, looked as if it had been stitched out of the air itself. An embroidered scarlet bodice heightened the curves of her perfect figure. Primroses had been woven into her hair by a stylist who'd arrived breathless in our crowded flat, adding to the chaos of last-minute preparations. The highlight of her outfit was the exquisitely modelled wings that a costume-designer friend had made especially. As Evie moved around they caught the candlelight, sending out rainbows of cascading light.

She was every definition of female beauty. My Evie. My soon-to-be wife.

Energy swirled through my chest as we stood in front of everyone, gazing at each other. I was only dimly aware of our friends. All I could really see was the face of my soulmate before me.

I realised that Sarah had just finished the reading that we'd chosen from *The Alchemist* by Paulo Coelho, about love being the language of the world. It had left everyone in bits. Now Jane was turning to me and nodding. The time had come for Evie and me to share our vows.

I felt a swirl of nerves, but the moment I looked into Evie's eyes, they dissolved away. I took a deep breath and began to read my speech. I'd poured my heart into it, but still I didn't feel it said everything that I felt for her.

'You know that feeling when you meet someone and it's as if you've known them your whole life?' I started. 'Well, it was exactly like that for me when I first met you, Evie. On the blind date that Sarah had set us up on, when I let you share my dessert – yes, I was that chivalrous –' a ripple of laughter passed around – 'I knew I'd found my best friend for life. For the first time in my life, a deep sense of peace and stillness filled me. Meeting you, Evie, felt like coming home.'

A smile filled Evie's face and she nodded.

'You are my pole star, a wonderful sassy woman who lights up even my greyest days, the strong woman who has always kept me on my toes and pushed me to be the best version of myself. You, Evie, are a woman who won't just happily dance with me in the puddles, but loves to stamp in them too.'

Over Evie's shoulder, I noticed Matt and Sarah wiping their eyes.

'In this crazy world of ours, you are my anchor in any of the storms that life can throw at us. I will forgive you your lack of love for spaghetti westerns and comic books – even if they are a perfectly valid art form.'

Another gentle flurry of laughter came from our friends.

'Despite those shortcomings, you light up every aspect of my life. Evie, you are my universe, you are my everything, the smile in my heart, the person I share my tears with, and my laughter. I will always be there for you throughout our adventure together. I intend to hold your hand and be yours for infinity plus a day. You are my everything. And…' I took a shuddering breath. 'Losing you will break me for ever.'

Several sobs came from our friends and tears suddenly ran down Evie's face as she cradled my hands in hers. She looked at me with such utter love that I felt my heart splintering.

But then she smeared away her tears and looked up into my eyes. 'Today, Adam, surrounded by our friends and family, who have helped shape who we are, I choose you to love as my husband in however many precious weeks life gives us to continue our dance together. To stand by your side, and sleep in your arms, as your wife. To keep you and hold you, comfort and protect you, for always and for ever, even when I am no longer here.'

I clenched my jaw in a desperate attempt to hold it together to the end of her speech.

She smiled at me even as tears ran down her cheeks. 'I will listen to you with compassion and understanding – and when I get this wrong I'll put it right. So, together let us build on this life together full of love, laughter and light, passion and adventure, so that our memories will always echo in your heart.' Her shoulders curled forward as she took a deep breath. 'And after I die, and when you slip the bounds of this world too, the stardust that makes up our bodies, blown like thistledown on the wind, will find each other across this cosmos. We will discover each other again, two souls entwined. There I will kiss you and say it has all been worth it, every moment of it, my love.'

I could barely see her through the curtain of my own tears. Sobbing, she pulled me to her and hung on. The walls holding back the emotion crumbled and everyone was weeping now, even Jane, as Evie stood on tiptoes and kissed me.

EVIE SPUN AROUND ME, her arm locked into mine as we danced to the Irish fiddle music the quartet was raucously playing. Couples blurred past us, laughing and whooping as the musicians upped the tempo. With a rising flourish of notes, their performance came to an end.

People put their hands in air and applauded, shouting, 'More, more!'

'I think that's our cue for a breather,' Evie said, towing me away between the couples.

'Thank god for that,' I said, clutching my sides. 'I don't know where you're getting your energy from, but I'm shattered.'

'Don't you worry, I'll be paying the price for all this tomorrow – with interest,' Evie replied.

A spike of concern shot through me. 'You should have said something.'

Evie shook her head. 'Absolutely not. I want my wedding day to the man I love to be perfect, and it is. But there is one last thing I need to do.' She took my hand and we slipped away from the others into the woods.

I smiled at her. 'If you're after a quickie, I'm not sure that's such a great idea with so many people around.'

She nudged my shoulder with hers. 'No, not that, but I am so seducing you later on.'

'I'll keep you to that.'

'Please do.'

We headed deeper into the woods along a pathway that had been lit with more of the jam-jar lights. As the music faded away behind us, for a moment I thought I could glimpse a fairy grotto between the trees. But then a clearing in the woods revealed itself. Hundreds of the jam-jar lights had been placed in a circle around an old sawn-off trunk. On top of that and wrapped with flowers was a wooden box.

'What's this?' I whispered, as though talking too loudly might make the whole scene vanish.

Evie's smile widened. 'Oh, you'll see.'

She led me by the hand through a pathway between the jam jars. A tawny owl with dappled brown feathers watched us from a nearby hornbeam tree, its large eyes blinking as we approached the box.

When we reached the tree stump I saw that the box had been carved with trees, stars woven in between their branches. A crescent moon adorned its lid.

Evie gestured towards it. 'I commissioned Matt to make this for me. And Sarah set up all the candles in secret so you wouldn't see it until now.'

'Well, if you wanted to surprise me, it's certainly worked.'

'Good.' She picked up the box and held it out to me. 'This is my wedding gift to you, Adam.'

'It's beautiful...but I thought we said we weren't getting gifts for each other. I didn't get you anything.'

She smiled at me. 'Would you please relax, Adam? You've given me so much already. And you don't understand; this box is just the wrapper – it's what's inside that really matters.'

I took the box from her, now completely intrigued, and put my finger on the ornate silver fastener to open it. But Evie placed her hand on mine and shook her head.

'No, not now. You're to open this when I'm gone.'

The candles guttered slightly in a sudden breeze and the shadows seemed to deepen outside the circle of candlelight.

A sense of unease washed over me. 'Don't talk like that.'

'Well, we should, Adam. It's the elephant in the room, or in this particular case, the woods. And as much fun as it's been to dance in the moonlight, we both know that our life together will be drawing to an end soon.'

My stomach dropped and I lowered my gaze to the floor. 'I can't live without you.'

Evie put her hand under my chin and made me look at her. 'You mustn't talk or think like that. Not ever, do you hear me? Life is such a precious gift and your part of this contract is to go out there and help to make this world a better place in whatever way you can.' She placed her hand over my heart. 'You are such a good man, Adam, and this world desperately needs people like you. Lean into your own fear to beat it and preach what you have discovered in these woods and open people's eyes to the wonder of it. Encourage them to do a better job of protecting this beautiful world of ours. Do you hear me?'

Standing before me with wings strapped to her bodice and a fierce look on her face, Evie looked more like an avenging angel than a woodland fairy in that moment.

I dragged my hand through my hair. 'You can be very scary when you want to be.'

'Good. Do you promise me then?'

'I do...'

'That's more like it. Now there's just one other thing I need to let you know. That box also contains my completed symphony.'

I stared at her. 'But if it's finished, we should be getting organised to have it performed, before...' My words trailed away. I couldn't bring myself to say it.

'Before I die,' Evie said, completing my sentence without flinching. 'No, it's my legacy. The music already lives in me – and maybe even in these very woods. I no longer need to hear it. This is my gift to you and the world. And when you hear it, I hope you'll remember this magical night and all the other magical memories we have created together.

'Oh god, Evie...' A sob broke from my lips.

She grabbed me and pulled me into the warmth of her love and I melted into her embrace.

CHAPTER 15

Four weeks later, the joy and celebration of our wedding day already seemed like a distant memory. The cancer had quickly strengthened its hold on Evie's body and spread to secondary sites, including her kidneys and even her brain.

I'd been forced to witness her life being stolen away, day by day, feeling as if somebody was slowly grinding my heart into a pulp in a mortar and pestle. The spark that made Evie who she was, was dimming, and darkness was closing in. There was nothing I could do to stop it.

Just over a fortnight ago, an ashen-faced Sarah had told us that Evie had only a matter of weeks. And there it was again, death – that word, brutal and so final.

Yet Evie had remained steadfast in her determination to stay at home rather than move into a hospice, though she had been bedridden for the last twelve days as her strength deserted her.

District nurses were normal fixtures of our days, coming in to check on Evie and administer a cocktail of painkillers. Each and every one of them swept into our lives like little glimmers of light in the growing gloom. All wonderful human beings, full of compassion and understanding, knowing what to say and do, and even more importantly a well-honed instinct about when not to say anything at all. They all did everything they could to make her palliative end-of-life care as comfortable as they could while still maintaining her dignity. And we both adored them for it.

Evie had effectively drawn up the drawbridge to nearly everybody in her life. All friends were restricted to emails – absolutely no visits or phone calls. She didn't want them to see or hear her this way, and I understood that. There were only a couple of exceptions. First, Sarah and Matt, who popped by regularly. Matt had tried to get me to go for a drink on numerous occasions, so I had someone to confide in, but I just couldn't bear to be away from Evie's side.

The other allowed guests were her parents. The more Lilly and James watched their daughter slipping away, the more their faces became haunted, expressions I often saw in my face in the mirror. Over the last week they'd been barely able to hide their pain and we'd heard them sobbing outside the house on the street where they thought we couldn't hear them. It broke Evie every time. A week ago, it had finally become too much for her. I'd sat on the edge of her bed while she'd told them what was in her heart.

'Mum, Dad, I love you so much, but I can't put you through this any more. I don't want you to see me slipping away like this. We need to say our goodbyes now.'

So I'd watched the most heart-breaking scene I'd ever witnessed: parents saying a final goodbye to their child.

Evie had held each of them as they'd sobbed. She'd whispered goodbye and held back her own tears, pouring the last of her emotional strength into her parents. And then they had gone, their masks shattering as grief tore them away. They left a void in the room where their love should have been. It was only then that Evie had at last allowed herself to fall apart and weep.

And I knew if Evie could have done, she'd have sent me away

too – to some faraway land to spare me the pain of what lay ahead. But there was no way that would ever happen.

Over the next few days, it felt as if I was standing on a beach, watching silent, flickering storm clouds over the ocean roll inexorably towards the land. Sarah had taken me briefly aside to explain that Evie had only a matter of days left now and to prepare myself. But how could I prepare myself for this? For the love of my life to be extinguished?

The district nurses had increased her morphine as the pain had begun to wrack her body, the cancer cells continuing to multiply, strengthening their hold on her. Evie's breathing became more laboured and now she had to wear an oxygen mask. Occasionally she'd pull it off to say something.

Once she said, 'If I came with an off switch, I'd be asking you to flick it right now.'

And part of me was right there with her, wanting to end her suffering. She'd even asked Sarah if she could top up her morphine levels so she could just slip peacefully away. But Sarah, pacing the room, had refused point-blank, her tear-filled eyes sliding away from Evie's gaze.

'That's not the way medical care works in this country,' she'd said, even though we all knew it would only be a kindness to someone with a terminal diagnosis.

No wonder so many people in similar situations chose to go abroad to countries such as Belgium where they could opt for voluntary euthanasia. Those countries got it. They understood it was much better to let the patient make a positive choice to die surrounded by compassion and love in their final moments.

And then finally, the day arrived…

It was the second week of September. I woke suddenly, something having jolted me from my sleep. The flat was dark but there was a hint of the coming dawn through the window. Evie had insisted the curtains be pulled back so she could gaze out at the view of Wytham Woods. A dark gash of red sliced across the horizon as if someone had taken a knife to the grey cloud-filled sky, now bleeding from the wound.

'Adam…' Evie said.

I got up from the inflatable mattress I'd set up at the base of the bed. Evie had found it increasingly uncomfortable to have me sleeping next to her.

Evie's breathing mask was off and she drew in a shaky breath.

'Are you okay?' I asked.

'Daft question…of the…century.' She managed a faint smile.

'You know what I mean…' I sat carefully beside her on the edge of the bed.

'Okay, I need you…to be strong.' Evie pulled up the mask and took a deep breath of oxygen.

A cold feeling filled my stomach. I gripped her hand in mine as she lowered her mask again, her eyes clinging to mine.

'One last thing…on my…bucket list.' Her fingers clamped on to my hand. 'Want…to die…under our mother tree today.' She let her head sink back into the pillow, but her fierce eyes still held mine, as if she was daring me to challenge her.

Something in my throat fluttered. 'You want to die up in Wytham? You want me to take you up there?'

She took another breath of oxygen and nodded.

The coldness in my stomach turned to ice and spread out from my core into the rest of my body. I gestured towards the morphine drip and the monitoring equipment. 'But you're hooked up to all this stuff.'

She pulled on the mask. 'Adam, do this for me.' Brow furrowing, she got hold of the morphine drip and, before I could stop her, pulled it out of her arm.

'Oh fuck!' I reached to the bedside cabinet for my phone. 'Don't worry – I'll get help and we'll get that drip put back in.'

But Evie grabbed my wrist with sudden strength and pulled my hand away from my phone, shaking her head. 'No!' Then she pulled off the sensor strapped to her finger. At once the numbers on the monitoring screen were replaced with dashes and warning bleeps.

Lines spidered around Evie's eyes as she forced herself into a sitting position. 'Not hooked up now…am I?'

I cradled her hands in mine. 'You can't do this.'

Evie shook her head. 'Yes…I…can.' She took a long breath, gesturing with her chin towards the bedside cabinet. 'In there is a letter…so you don't get into trouble with the police,' she said, her voice steadying.

Tears filled my eyes. 'Oh god, Evie, but I can't.'

She reached up to cup my face with her hand. 'I know how hard this will be for you…but please grant me this one last wish, Adam.'

I stared at this beautiful creature, this woman who was part of my own soul. All I wanted was to keep her safe, to keep her death at bay a little longer. But leaving this sanctuary would make my nightmare real.

Evie raised her chin towards the window.

I turned to see the slit of sunlight growing behind Wytham Woods, kissing its canopy crowns with amber. When I turned back to Evie she had her hands pressed together in an act of prayer.

And then I knew that I had to do this for her.

A sense of dizziness swept through me as I smeared my tears away with the back of my hand. 'Are you sure that this is what you really want?'

She took another gulp of the oxygen and looked deep into my eyes, into my very soul. 'Yes, Adam, it is.'

~

As the grey sky shifted towards the copper tones of the strengthening dawn, I drove as deep as I could into the woods along the mud track that was only normally used by the vehicles of the team who looked after Wytham.

Evie sat beside me, wrapped in enough layers for an Arctic explorer.

The track's ruts grew deeper and we crept along in the car, mud splatters spraying up the side of the vehicle and across the windows. Soon the inevitable happened. With a scream, the front wheels spun free in the wet ground and we came to a shuddering halt.

Evie turned towards me, blinking, her mouth hidden behind the mask I'd connected to a smaller portable oxygen cylinder.

I nodded, driving my fingernails into my palms to hold back the tears. 'Don't worry, I'll carry you the rest of the way.'

I climbed out of the car and shouldered the rucksack from the back that I'd packed with another fleece for Evie in case she needed it. Anything to try to make this awful situation a little bit more comfortable for her. Then I took the picnic blanket and slung it over my shoulder. As I closed the boot, I leant on it, dropping my head between my arms as I tried to gather myself.

I could do this. I had to, for Evie's sake.

I took a deep breath, headed around to the passenger door and opened it.

Evie gazed up at me, her eyes watery, her breathing shallow.

I crouched before her. 'I'll ask you one final time if you're certain you want me to do this?'

She nodded. 'Yes…I…am,' she replied, her voice muffled by the mask.

I pinched the bridge of my nose and squeezed my eyes shut for a second. 'Okay…'

My nostrils flared as I looked at her again with my best attempt at a reassuring smile. Then I took her oxygen bottle and, careful not to detach the clear tube connected to it, slipped it into my rucksack. Finally, I reached across her, unhooked her seat belt and gently lifted her out of the car. Just as I had been back at the flat when I'd lifted her from the bed, I was struck by how light Evie had become as her body succumbed to the cancer. It felt as if I were lifting a child as I stood up with her in the crook of my arms. I nudged the door shut with my foot and we set off into the woods.

Evie nuzzled her head into my chest as I carried her. As we moved between the trees, I could hear things scurrying away into the undergrowth. Evie squeezed my hand and raised her chin towards a rabbit on the path dead ahead of us. It sat upright, its head swivelling towards us as we approached.

Evie watched it with wide, hungry eyes, drinking in the moment. Then, in a flurry of movement, the rabbit and half a dozen other white tails – its companions I hadn't noticed – disappeared into the bushes too.

'God…so…love…this place,' she whispered.

I couldn't squeeze out any words past the boulder filling my throat. So instead I just squeezed her hand and nodded.

At last we reached the clearing, the faint mesh network sensors' LED lights stretching away around us like green fireflies. My experiment, still running, had been maintained by my students, although I hadn't looked at any of the data since I'd last been here.

I unhooked the picnic blanket from my shoulder and dropped it on the ground, nudging it into position with my foot, and then gently lowered Evie down. She immediately curled on to her side in a foetal position, resting her head on the rising lump of one of the roots.

She gazed up at me and pulled her mask off. 'Thank you,' she said in a small voice.

I lay down next to Evie and kissed her gently on the mouth.

Her eyes, the life in them beginning to dim, held mine. 'Don't…forget…to open…the box,' she said between rasping breaths. 'It…will…help.'

I nodded as tears stung my eyes. 'I promise.'

'Good...'

The burnished haze of red in the sky started to strengthen as we held on to each other. Evie gazed over my shoulder, the sunrise painting her ashen skin with gold. I cradled my body around her, giving her my warmth, as if I could save her with my life.

'Oh...my,' she whispered.

I looked back over my shoulder to see a doe standing less than ten metres away, gazing at us. Silhouetted against the sun peaking between the trees, her fur glowed with a golden halo. Her eyes contained no fear as she looked at us and I could see a deep intelligence behind them, maybe even an understanding about what was happening here. But how could that be?

'So...beautiful...' Evie said.

I turned back to her, holding her close, feeling her heart against mine. I could hear the gentle breathing of the deer nearby, as if it had decided to stand guard over us.

The deep stillness of the woods began to reach into me as I held Evie. I felt an impossible sense of serenity take hold, as though this was the perfect way to mark the ending of a life.

Evie gasped and her eyes began to flutter as I heard the deer moving quietly away behind us.

Fear rose up through me as I pulled her closer. 'Evie, please don't leave me!'

'I'm...sorry...' she replied. And then her eyes rolled up into her head as an awful gasping sound came from the back of her throat. Her head sank on to the root.

'No, no, no!' I shouted.

At that same moment, all the mesh sensor lights flicked from green to red and warbled out a shrill alarm cry that spread across the woods.

I ignored them and clasped Evie by the shoulders, but felt only the shocking stillness of her. I pressed my fingertips to her neck to feel for a pulse and found none. Her body had become a husk.

And, just like that, my beautiful Evie, a chunk of my own soul, was gone.

Raw, searing pain flooded my body as I clasped her to me. I tipped my head back as my soul shattered and I screamed, a primordial cry of loss from the very bottom of my being that echoed throughout the woods.

CHAPTER 16

I shook as we stood in the crematorium chapel, my gaze locked on to the wooden coffin that contained Evie's body. As if that wasn't heart-breaking enough, Sarah had draped Evie's fairy wedding dress over it. If anything was the perfect metaphor for this tragedy, this would be it. Life, love and death.

It had felt totally surreal when I'd first entered the chapel as one of the coffin bearers. Matt flanked me on the opposite side and two of the funeral team were behind us, as we'd carried her coffin in and lowered it on to the stand at the front. The pitying gazes that had tracked our progress inside felt almost tangible and the hairs on the back of my neck rose.

Despite feeling the weight of her as we'd brought the coffin in, part of me couldn't accept that she really was inside it. As I stood in the front row of the chapel, I found myself rocking forward on the balls of my feet, fighting the instinct to rush to the coffin and rip the lid off to prove to everyone that she wasn't inside. But part of me knew the truth, even if I wanted to deny it.

I tried to focus on the words of the song in the service programme, but my mind kept sliding over them, unable to hang on.

This had been exactly what the last couple of weeks had been like, a blur that I could barely remember... I recalled Lilly and James falling apart when I'd told them the awful news. Then a succession of grieving faces as friends and family had called around. Standing in our bathroom sobbing as I held Evie's toothbrush in my hand and ringing Sarah and Matt in the middle of the night. They'd come around straight away to comfort me through that lonely, dark time.

Amid the tsunami of emotions, one memory was crystal clear: when the police had come to interview me at home. The first thing they'd told me was that the coroner had confirmed death by natural causes. They'd spoken to Dr Reece, who'd told them that taking her up to the woods would in no way have accelerated her death. If anything, my actions had probably eased her passing. Evie's letter saying that it had been her decision and not mine had helped confirm my version of events. So the detectives, a man and a woman, had told me no charges would be brought. The female detective had even hugged me as she'd left.

Since Evie's death I hadn't been in any fit state to resume my classes. But the college had continued to be fantastic, signing me off for as long as I needed. My colleague, Geoff, had taken over my classes until I was able to return.

So my days had blurred into nights, when I could barely sleep. I became a husk of the man I'd once been.

The song drew to a close. It was only then that I realised it was 'Imagine' by John Lennon, one of Evie's favourites.

I was dimly aware of all the people crammed into the chapel, a sea of mostly grey and black, despite the request that they wore something bright and happy. It was something that Evie had told me she wanted in one of the many conversations that had splintered my heart in the weeks leading up to her death, making that inevitable moment more real. I was sure those wearing the usual funeral uniform thought they were being respectful, but I knew Evie would have hated it.

The few that had abided by her wish stood out like exotic flowers in that drab monotone landscape. I was wearing the brightest thing in my wardrobe: a cobalt-blue shirt that Evie had always loved. On my left side, Lilly and James had tried to follow her wishes. James was sporting a vivid emerald-green tie and Lilly had a pink silk scarf around her neck, which Evie had given to her as a Christmas present the previous year.

But we all paled in comparison to what Matt and Sarah were wearing. Matt was in a waistcoat so bright it would have put Joseph's technicolor dreamcoat to shame. Beside him, Sarah's sequinned dress glittered like a disco ball. I adored them both for it.

The two of them had been my rock over the last couple of weeks, doing everything they could to support me, along with James and Lilly, despite coping with their own grief. They both looked as if they'd aged ten years since they'd lost Evie. There was so much I wanted to say about their gorgeous daughter, but whenever I tried, the words got lost somewhere in the empty echoing tunnels of my soul.

Matt nudged me slightly in the side and opened his waistcoat a fraction like a guy in a market trying to sell me some knock-off Rolexes. But instead of watches, he gestured to the hip flask in his red silk-lined internal pocket. He didn't say a word, but instead just raised both eyebrows a fraction at me.

I nodded and Matt slipped the flask over. Sarah caught the movement out of the corner of her eye and winced as her eyes zeroed in on the alcohol being passed between us.

As discreetly as I could with the eyes of at least a hundred people on my back, I took a nip of what turned out to be body-warmed neat vodka.

The tremor inside me subsided slightly after the first swig. It was helping; anything to numb the icy void inside me. I took a longer gulp, this time no longer caring what anyone thought.

But then I caught Lilly's downturned expression as she and

James watched me. She looked at the coffin and closed her eyes. It was as if she'd just shouted at me, 'You're letting Evie down, Adam. Get a fucking grip!'

The muscles tightened across my chest. I dropped my head and slipped the flask into my trouser pocket. Matt didn't say a word, but patted my arm.

Jane stood at the lectern, the same woman who'd married us such a short time ago. As her gaze rose from her notes, she looked directly at me and smiled. I couldn't handle the compassion in her eyes and slid my gaze away from her back to Evie's coffin.

How could a woman so vital be caged within that wooden box? Evie was a bird who should be flying free through the sky. How could she be gone? How could she not be waiting for me just outside this chapel, ready to jump on me as I emerged saying, 'Gotcha!' I couldn't believe it, yet I knew it deep down. Evie's body was inside that coffin and she really was lost to me for ever.

I became aware that Jane was talking and probably had been for some time. She nodded towards Sarah who, cradling a piece of paper in her hand, stood up and headed towards the lectern as Jane stepped aside. Sarah smoothed out the paper in front of her and I found myself looking at her in a way that I never had before. In the sweep of her features, I could see the echoes of Evie's face. In that moment, the similarities between the sisters hit me.

Sarah raised her face to us…to me. She opened her mouth to speak, but nothing came out. She gave a slight shake of her head. With a deep breath, she tried again.

'This is a poem by Charles Péguy, translated from French, called "I'm Just the Other Side of the Road".'

Sarah gazed across the chapel and straight into my eyes.

'Death is nothing, I only went to the next room. I am me. You are you.'

My hands started to grow sweaty as she continued.

'What I was for you, I still am. Give me the name you always gave me; talk to me as you always have. Do not use a different tone; do not

look solemn or sad. Keep laughing about what made us laugh together. Pray, smile, think of me, pray for me. May my name be pronounced at home as it has always been, without emphasis of any kind, without a trace of shadow.'

I tried to swallow but I was finding it hard to breathe.

'Life means all that it ever was. The cord is not cut. Why would I be out of your mind, simply because I'm out of your sight? I'm not far, just on the other side of the road. You see, everything is fine.'

I glanced across at Evie's coffin and heat flushed through my body.

I turned back to Sarah, my teeth bared. 'How can everything be bloody fine? Evie is lying dead in that damn box!'

Next to me, Lilly bit back a sob and turned her head into James's chest. He hung on to her and shook his head at me.

But I was no longer in control as wild grief rose through me. I pushed past Evie's parents and headed up to the coffin. I grabbed her fairy wedding dress and held it to my face, my hot tears staining it as I tried to breathe in her scent. But there was none of her there, just a hint of dry-cleaning chemicals.

I held it up to the people watching me with wide eyes. I was the poor idiot husband who was losing his mind. 'Can't you see? It's never going to be all right!'

I caught the tears streaming down Sarah's face as she watched me from the lectern.

Matt was heading towards me, arms outstretched as if he were trying to corner a wild animal. There should have been hostility in the eyes of everyone else, but all I could see was compassion.

It felt like bands of steel dug into the flesh around my chest. I dropped the dress back on to the coffin.

Matt placed his arm gently on mine. 'Come on, mate…'

I spun around. 'Leave me alone, Matt!' I strode up the aisle between the mourners, ignoring all of them.

I slammed my way out through the doors, taking a gasp of the chilly winter air. Fast footsteps came from behind and I glanced back to see Matt hurrying after me. I headed towards my car that I'd insisted on using rather than riding in the hearse and being gawped in at by strangers on the street. I pulled my remote out and unlocked the vehicle with a blink of its indicators.

'Adam, stop, you're in no state to drive!' Matt called as he began running after me.

But I jumped inside and slammed the door shut. As I started the car up, Matt slid to a stop in front of the bonnet.

'Adam, please stop,' he shouted through the windscreen.

But I could barely hear him over the roar of my grief. I had to get out of there, to get away from Evie's body lying in that box, to get away from everyone.

I pressed the accelerator to the floor and the car surged forward. Matt just had enough time to leap aside. I glanced back in my rear-view mirror to see him watching me go. Then he slowly shook his head and lowered his eyes as he traipsed back towards the chapel and the other mourners.

~

My eventual destination hadn't been a conscious decision. I'd just driven at high speed, racing through the lanes of Oxfordshire and ignoring the buzz of my mobile phone in my pocket. I'd only realised I was driving like a lunatic when I almost lost control around a blind bend. That had frightened me enough to slow down. Then, as if on autopilot, I found myself driving towards Wytham Woods.

I parked up by the lodge and began wandering through the woods, barely aware of the icy chill.

My phone buzzed again and this time I did glance at the screen. There were ten missed calls from Matt and five from Sarah, plus numerous texts that I didn't bother to read. I pressed the phone's power button until the screen flicked to black and I pocketed it. I just needed everyone to leave me alone.

I let my feet lead me, my breathing shallow.

The stillness of winter had settled over the woods, the harsh calls of the rooks the only bird sounds to be heard. The bare branches were silhouetted against the leaden grey sky like hundreds of gnarled fingers. These woods had once been beautiful, but with Evie gone they were nothing to me now.

I found myself approaching Arwen as if approaching a grave, my heart growing heavy. I gazed down at the spot where Evie's life force had faded away to leave an empty body behind – a body that right now was being turned into ash by the crematorium's incinerator.

I sank to my knees and placed my hand against the trunk of the ancient oak. 'Why did you have to leave me alone, Evie?'

My breath clouded the air as my tears came hot and fast.

'I can't do this without you,' I said between sobs. The world became hazy as my vision was clouded by my tears.

A breeze started to scrape the branches of the tree together like dozens of claws. Darkness seemed to creep in around me – a dark tide that tugged at my limbs, my mind, drawing me into its embrace of despair. I became aware of the throbbing of my heart as the breeze strengthened between the trees.

The wind moaned through the branches, changing and becoming two syllables, 'Ad...am,' a faint woman's voice said.

My scalp prickled. This was like that time I'd had the strange dream here. But now I was very much awake. So what was this then? My mind playing tricks on me? Or had Sarah and Matt come looking for me in the one obvious place I'd be?

I stood up and turned around, slowly scanning the trees, but no one was there.

'Adam...' the voice repeated.

This time my heart clenched. It was Evie.

I tried to call out but couldn't speak. The logical part of my brain knew it couldn't be her. This had to be the beginning of full-blown breakdown as I tipped over the edge into the black pit of madness.

The wind screamed around me now, dead leaves rising in flurries.

'Adam,' Evie's voice said from within the maelstrom.

I stood, frozen to the spot, my heart hammering. At last I managed to speak. 'But none of this can be real.'

The leaves began to flow into patterns of a person…a woman who was reaching out for me. And it was as if the world in that moment was fading away and I was stepping through some sort of looking glass into the other side.

'Evie!' I cried out.

'Adam, Adam, Adam…' her voice said, seeming to come from everywhere at the same time.

My thoughts tilted, nothing real any longer, my heart racing so hard that a pain lanced through it. Fear exploded through me as I stared at the apparition carved from leaves that stood before me. None of this made any sense. It was the wild vision of a madman. I turned away and ran, running as fast as I could to get away from this waking nightmare.

Time became meaningless, a blurred impression of trunks hurtling past as I sprinted away. The real world only snapped back into focus when I jumped into the car and sped away into the growing storm.

CHAPTER 17

The half-empty whisky tumbler glowed against the reading light as I held it up to examine its contents. I tilted the glass, sending small waves across its amber ocean…an ocean in which I'd been slowly drowning myself for the last seven days since Evie's funeral. I needed oblivion and alcohol gave me exactly that. Anything to numb the mind-crushing grief that had shattered my soul.

I sat alone in the flat, the reading light the only source of illumination in the darkness. Dirty plates I'd left piled high in the sink cast mountain-range shadows against the wall. I'd not even been able to find the will to put them in the dishwasher. Take-away boxes brought to me by the Oxford home-delivery bike couriers littered every surface. Discarded dirty clothes covered the floor.

I took a long slug of my whisky, welcoming the bite of heat into my body. I felt chilled to the core, despite turning the thermostat up to max.

Through the winter darkness of early evening outside, I could just make out Wytham Woods silhouetted against the skyline. I shuddered, still not fully understanding what had happened. The most logical explanation – and the one I clung on to – was that I'd been so broken up with grief that I'd hallucinated the whole thing. Evie's voice couldn't have been anything other than a trick of my mind. I had obviously been so distraught by the funeral that part of my subconscious had conjured her up to ease my pain. A psychiatrist could probably have a field day with me right now.

I took another sip of the whisky and felt the ice inside me melt a fraction.

The fact I could lose it like that – a scientist with a supposedly rational mind – had scared me more than anything else. To stare down into the abyss of madness for a second had been a moment too long for me.

I stood up and crossed to the window to look out at the dark tree-topped hillside. My research work lay abandoned up there. It would stay there for ever as far as I was concerned. I'd ignored my students' emails about whether they should continue to maintain the mesh sensor network. How could I ever go back when I was barely hanging on to my sanity as it was? If I heard Evie's voice again, it would be the end of me.

I pulled the blind down, making a mental note to never open it again so I wouldn't have to look out at the woods.

I was surrounded by memories of Evie. From her coats hanging by the door to her favourite mugs in the cupboard that I just couldn't use. Her toothbrush still stood next to mine, Sarah and Matt encouraging me to throw it away. But every single item was a link to her, something to be cherished. Under all my debris, the flat was a shrine to the woman I loved, even if that shrine was currently being neglected by its guardian.

My gaze fell upon the engraved box on the desk. I still hadn't been able to bring myself to open it. I knew it would shatter my heart all over again as she'd no doubt filled it with things that she thought would help...including her symphony. But to hear even one note from that would take me straight back to the opening bars she'd played for the first time back in the woods. No, I couldn't open it. Not yet. Maybe never.

The answer machine light was blinking an accusing red, as if shouting, 'Listen to me, you stupid bastard.' Several days ago I'd muted the damned thing so I couldn't hear the endless messages of support from friends, all trying to reach out to me to help. But what could anyone have really done? There was a vast hole in the centre of my being and nothing could fill that space.

I hadn't made a conscious decision to withdraw from the world; it had just worked out that way. Increasingly I found I couldn't even face Matt and Sarah; it only made me think of all the happy times the four of us had spent together. Too many memories that would destroy me. So this flat was the extent of my reality now, the rest of the world a haze of darkness beyond its windows. But even within the safety of the flat, the pain – raw, brutal – was a living monster that stalked me, triggered by the slightest thing that would make the beast roar with grief.

Sometimes it was the strands of Evie's hair in her hairbrush; other times the abandoned mouldy bananas on the side she had used for her smoothies. A million echoes of my soulmate were everywhere in this flat, all waiting to trip me into an endless cycle of anguish.

I drained my glass and was heading back to the sofa and the whisky bottle when the door intercom buzzed.

I froze. I hadn't ordered a takeaway and this was too late for any other sort of delivery.

The door buzzed again. I licked my dry lips. It had to be a friend – specifically Sarah or Matt, or maybe both. They'd continually tried to see me throughout the week, most likely because I hadn't returned their calls. I hadn't let them in then and I couldn't now.

I refilled my tumbler from the whisky bottle and took a long swig. A warm, woozy feeling softened the swirl of panic spinning inside me. I started to relax when the buzzer didn't go again.

Whomever it was had obviously given up. But then I heard a conversation drifting up from the bottom of the stairwell and immediately recognised Sarah's voice. She was talking to Mrs Jenkins, who must have buzzed her in.

My heart became sluggish as the sound of footsteps on the stairs grew louder. I jumped as the inevitable knock on the door came – sharp, loud and meaning business.

'Adam, I know you're in there, so you might as well let me in,' Sarah said.

I stared at the door, willing her to go away.

'Adam, please. I just need to see with my own eyes that you're doing okay. Evie made me and Matt promise that we'd keep an eye out for you after she was gone. And that's a bit bloody hard when you won't see or speak to us.'

I took another sip of whisky.

'Come on, Adam. Don't make my promise to Evie a lie.'

I hung my head. Even in my state, Sarah understood me well enough to know how to get through to me.

As I headed towards the door, I swayed slightly on my feet and had to concentrate hard to stay balanced. It was only then that I realised just how much I'd had to drink.

I reached the door and unlocked it. As I pulled it open, the bottom of the door slid into the pile of envelopes Mrs Jenkins had carried up from my mailbox downstairs and posted underneath. The mail heaped up into a small landslide around my feet as I opened the door only a tiny amount – not wide enough to let my visitor in.

Sarah stared at me through the gap, pursing her lips. 'My god, Adam, you look as rough as hell.'

'Oh, I feel far worse than that.'

'I bet you do. So can I come in?'

'What if I said no?'

'Then I'd probably ignore you and do it anyway.'

'Okay,' I sighed, stepping aside with a flourish of my hand and slightly dipping my head as if I were a footman of a princess's royal carriage.

Sarah forced the door open farther, jamming into the letters, and squeezed through the gap, closing it behind her. She frowned as her eyes swept like searchlights over the room, taking in the carnage left by a man who no longer cared. But she didn't say anything, probably guessing, correctly, that I didn't need any lectures right now.

She shrugged her coat off and hung it over Evie's cagoule.

I flinched and had to stop myself telling Sarah she couldn't put her coat there. Instead, I hunted through the sink for a glass, swilled it out and handed it to her.

She took it from me and sat on the sofa, patting the seat next to her. 'Okay, Adam, we need to talk.'

I grabbed the whisky bottle and, without asking her, filled her glass almost to the top. She grimaced as I went to refresh my own.

I raised my tumbler and clinked it to hers. 'To absent friends.'

'To Evie,' Sarah replied in a small voice.

'Amen to that.' I took a large gulp of the whisky.

Sarah took a small sip and placed her glass on the coffee table among piles of takeaway cartons. She angled her knees towards me and tilted her head to one side, just like Evie used to do.

I felt a twist in my heart at how even mannerisms were similar in the two sisters.

'So how are you coping, Adam?' Sarah asked.

I raised my shoulders and gestured around the flat. 'I think you can probably work that out for yourself.'

'Yes, I probably can. You do know we've all been going out of our minds with worry.'

'I just need to be left alone, Sarah. There is nothing anyone can say or do to bring Evie back.'

Lines radiated around Sarah's eyes as she squeezed them shut. Then she opened them again and took a deep breath. 'Adam, I know that as much as you do. You lost your wife and I lost my younger sister.'

A pain filled the back of my throat. 'Sorry, Sarah. How are you doing?'

'Badly, to be honest. I miss her so much. I'm just trying to get through this as best as I can.'

I nodded, drained the last of my whisky and refilled my glass. I offered the bottle to Sarah but she shook her head. 'So is this the part where you give me a lecture?'

'Yes. If it's tough love you need, then that's exactly what I'll give you. You can't shut yourself away from life like this, Adam. And I hate to lay the Evie guilt trip on you, but can you imagine how upset with you she'd be if she saw you letting yourself fall apart like this?'

'And right there is the problem, Sarah. She isn't here to see it and I –' I flapped my hand to indicate the state of the flat – 'I've regressed to a caveman. Worse still, I think I'm losing my mind.'

She reached over and patted my back. 'I'd be worried about you if you weren't going at least a little bit crazy right now. We all are. I've found myself dialling her mobile just to listen to her voice on her answering service – not once but a hundred times.'

'That sounds pretty normal from where I'm sitting right now.'

'Ah, but I didn't stop there. I've left her long rambling messages as though she were still alive. Anyway, my point is that going through the madness of grief is perfectly normal.'

I thought of hearing Evie's voice in the woods, but that was a whole other level of crazy that I wasn't going to offer up just yet.

I shrugged. 'I guess so.'

Sarah nodded and took a sip of the whisky. She pulled a face. 'Neat so isn't normally my speed.'

'Sorry, but there's only hard liquor in this flat now.'

Her gaze narrowed on me a fraction. 'I see... Please tell me you've been eating properly?'

'Surviving on takeaways as you can probably tell. Okay, so it isn't necessarily a balanced diet, but at least I'm eating.'

'And what about getting out of this flat?'

I shook my head. 'Not since the day of the funeral. I've been hunkering down in this cave trying to sort my head out.'

'And how is that strategy working out for you?'

Her blue eyes pierced mine with an intensity that told me I couldn't lie. 'Badly, Sarah.'

She leant towards me. 'I know everything is so raw right now, but have you considered any bereavement counselling?'

I shook my head. 'I couldn't cope with that. Even mentioning her name can set me off.'

'Yes, I can imagine. But it could really help you, perhaps a bit later down the line. In the meantime, you need to let your friends back into your life. Everyone is ready to pitch in – there are enough of us to supply you with home-cooked food to avoid you having any bloody takeaways for at least a year.'

I shook my head, managing a faint smile. 'Later maybe, but I'm not up to facing anyone yet.'

Sarah sighed and reached out and squeezed my arm. 'You do know you mean everything to Matt and me. I know how crap it's been for me, so I only begin to understand what you're going through.'

'If I'm honest, like utter shit.' I took another large slug of whisky.

Lines ridged across Sarah's forehead. 'Have you been doing a lot of that?' she said, gesturing towards my glass.

'It helps get me through the days and the long nights.'

She shook her head. 'Maybe, but as props go, it's an awful one. If anything, booze will make you feel worse in the long run.'

I shrugged. 'I'm not worried about the long run. I just need to make the pain go away now.'

Sarah drew her teeth over her lip. 'I could write you a

prescription for some tranquillisers to get you over this hardest part?'

'No, booze is fine for now. But thanks for the offer.'

She sighed. 'You don't have to go through this alone, Adam.' She squeezed my arm.

The warmth of her touch felt soothing. Human contact. But that small gesture acted as a trigger and my grief – sudden, shocking – was once again rising through me. I started to sob, sucking in lungfuls of air.

Sarah pulled me into a hug. 'God, this is all so bloody unfair.'

Her body felt so warm against me, as if I'd just wandered in out of the snow to stand in front of a fire.

'You poor broken lovely man,' she whispered into my ear, before pulling away and gazing at me, her face full of understanding.

I stared back at her through the film of my tears. Sarah's eyes were cut from the same crystal as Evie's, the sweep of high cheekbones identical too. Even the same lines of concern radiated from her eyes as she scrunched them up. So similar in so many ways to my Evie...

Something within me took over without conscious thought. Just need. I hooked my hands around Sarah's shoulders, pulling her towards me. Before she had a chance to react, I was pressing my mouth hard against hers, kissing her, trying to draw her warmth into my soul.

Sarah's hands were on my chest and she gently pushed me away. 'Adam, stop this. You don't know what you're doing.'

But the monster of my grief had taken me over and my hands started to slide up her back inside her shirt.

Her gentle push became a shove. 'Stop this, Adam!' She was on her feet and rushing to the door, grabbing her coat from the hook.

I watched her go, not moving as my head swam.

She opened the door and stared back at me. 'Adam, I need to go now.'

Thoughts rolled around my head in a confusion of emotion and alcohol. 'Evie, I'm sorry.'

Sarah jerked as if I'd physically struck her.

'Sorry…confused…' I slurred.

With a shake of her head, Sarah stepped out of the door and pulled it closed behind her.

I dropped my head into my hands. What the fuck had I done?

CHAPTER 18

My self-imposed prison sentence in my flat extended across the weeks. Gradually, one by one, people stopped bothering to contact me. Lilly and James tried a few more times, but finally seemed to have given up too. Not surprisingly, Sarah nor Matt hadn't contacted me since that awful night when I'd made that clumsy move on her. Sarah had obviously told Matt exactly what had happened and now neither of them wanted anything to do with me. And who could have blamed them? Certainly not me.

I cringed whenever I thought about that night. I could have put it down to the booze, but if someone had tried to use it to excuse themselves with me, I would have given them the look and probably a lot more besides. No, the truth was that I'd lost myself for a second, not caring about anything or anyone other than my own world of hurt. I had sought emotional oblivion with Sarah in a moment of madness. But I had stepped so far over the line I'd no doubt destroyed two of the most important friendships in my life.

I hated the person that I'd become.

Now my days were spent in an endless cycle of grief, emptiness and self-recrimination.

There was a retro prog song that Matt had introduced me to during uni, which become my anthem now: 'Comfortably Numb'. The lyrics said it all – about a guy using drugs to keep the world at bay. They might as well have been singing about me, just swap the drugs for alcohol. But now it didn't even seem to be able to take the edge off my pain. I was like a hamster on its wheel, spinning faster and faster and going exactly nowhere.

It didn't help that Evie's box was still sitting on the study desk, accusing me of cowardice every time I passed it. Even covering it with a tea towel hadn't really helped. I'd tried to open it a few times, but had experienced a full-blown panic attack each and every time.

So my hermit existence had taken hold. From my attic window I'd become a spectator, watching the flow of life in the streets of Oxford below. At some point the weeks had tipped over into December and now the Christmas lights on the high street peeked between the buildings in the distance. Life went on for everyone else.

But over the last few days, an itch had slowly taken hold in my mind, a realisation that I couldn't carry on like this. That had been underlined when I found myself in a full-blown rant at the smug breakfast TV presenter making some inane comment about some wannabe celebrity in the latest reality series. It was then that I realised I needed to reboot myself and that started with looking at my laptop for the first time in for ever.

I dragged the entire contents of my inbox straight to a *To Be Read Later* folder and discovered that it was the second Wednesday of December, according to the calendar – the penultimate week of term before the colleges closed for Christmas. Thursdays were my lecture days.

The next day I rose at 6 a.m., showered and even had a go at attacking my unruly beard with a pair of scissors. The man that stared back at me from the mirror of the bathroom cabinet, despite the hollowed-out eyes, actually looked vaguely human.

I wasn't up to driving anywhere, so I decided to ring for a taxi.

When the driver finally pulled up outside, I already had my jacket on and case in hand. I headed for the door, but paused, staring at it.

Come on, Adam, you can do this...

I took a deep breath, placed my hand on the door handle and opened it. As I stepped out on to the landing, a distinct swirl of vertigo spun through me. My heart thudded in unison with my steps as I headed down the stairs, the drumbeat of a person heading towards their executioner. But I forced myself to carry on. I needed to do this. I needed to get control of myself.

I'd almost reached the bottom of the stairs when Mrs Jenkins's flat door opened and she appeared with some milk bottles in her hand. Her grey eyes snapped towards me, her fingers touching her partly open lips. Then she blinked as she attempted to rally from her surprise.

'Adam...' Her mouth opened and closed again as she obviously attempted to work out the right thing to say to the grieving madman from upstairs.

'I'm going out to give a lecture,' I said, heading her off.

'Oh, I see. Well, wrap up warm, it's icy out there.'

I gestured to the winter jacket I was already wearing.

'Yes...silly me.' Her face softened. 'Adam, I just wanted to say how sorry I am, and if there's anything I can do...'

'Yes, thank you, Mrs Jenkins.' I gave her my best attempt at a smile and rushed past her to the door.

The world felt like a sledgehammer smashing into my brain as I stepped outside. A cyclist sped around the square, vying with a white van for position on the road. The pavements seemed to be crowded with half the population of Oxford in my fevered mind, although in reality there were probably just a couple of dozen people. But in that moment it felt as if every set of eyes were on me.

A flurry of blue tits flew among the trees in the park. They began chattering to each other, a reassuring sound of the woods. I felt myself surfacing from the chaos assaulting my imagination.

I blinked hard. No one was actually paying any attention to me at all. I took a deep breath.

You have to do this, Adam.

The taxi driver looked through his lowered window at me and I raised my chin. 'Christ Church college?' the guy asked.

I nodded and climbed into the back.

Please may this guy not want to tell me about the state of the country.

Thankfully the driver seemed content to gaze through the windscreen, lost in his own inner world like most people these days.

My hands clawed my leather case as I held it across me like a protective shield. Around us the busy streets of Oxford slipped past. I jigged my foot on the floor. Trying to slow my breathing, I closed my eyes.

Minutes, or perhaps hours later – I had no idea in my tightly wound state – the driver spoke again.

'Here we are, sir,' the man said.

I opened my eyes to see the gates to Christ Church next to us. I paid the driver and made my way towards the college. I'd barely stepped in through the main doors when someone called my name out from behind me.

'Hey, Adam, I didn't know you were coming in today,' a man's voice said.

I turned to see Geoff, the senior lecturer who had taken over my work during my leave of absence.

'I thought it was time,' I said.

'Yes...' His words trailed away just as Mrs Jenkins's had.

I felt a pang of sympathy for Geoff. After all, what could you say to someone whose life had just been shattered?

'I need to get back to my old routines. Giving my lectures will help,' I said, filling in the growing uncomfortable pause.

Geoff dragged his hand through his thinning grey hair. 'Are you sure, Adam? I'm more than happy to cover the last two lectures for this term. Why don't you catch your breath properly and start again in January? Take a long Christmas break?'

Christmas – the time of the year that had meant everything to Evie. She had even insisted on us leaving out stockings for Santa, both of which she would fill in the middle of night while she thought I was still sleeping. Her enthusiasm for mulled wine, decorating the tree and listening to carols from King's on the radio while she made homemade stollen was what made Christmas for me. Without her, it would be full of shadows.

I shook my head. 'No, it will be good for me to get back into the saddle sooner rather than later.'

Geoff tugged his ear. 'If you say so. But if you change your mind, I'm more than happy to step in. Meanwhile, try to not push yourself too hard.' He reached out and awkwardly patted my arm. This was a great show of affection from the guy known around the college for being the most reserved man on the planet.

That simple act of empathy brought a lump to my throat. 'I'll do my best.'

Not quite looking him in the eye, I turned and headed away quickly along the corridor.

Before me in the lecture theatre, the students' faces glowed from the light of their laptops. It was hard not to notice that their attention had been fixated on me for the last five minutes and not the slides of my presentation on the screen behind me. It was even harder to ignore the whispered conversations. It wasn't difficult to work out what they were talking about, based on what had happened when I'd first entered that room.

I'd been inundated as student after student had stepped forward to offer their condolences. Many of the women had hugged me. I'd done my best to meet each person with a fixed smile and what I hoped came across as polite indifference, because anything more and I would have lost it.

I had to get through this and get my life back on track in any way I could. That was what Evie would have wanted me to do…

I referred to my notes and cleared my throat. 'So, in addition to the mycorrhizal networks, there is research that suggests the trees also can transmit pheromones to communicate with each other. For example, when giraffes start eating the leaves of an acacia tree, it emits ethylene gas – basically a distress signal. When neighbouring acacias detect this, they start producing excess tannins in their leaves that can sicken and even kill the giraffes…'

A man's hand rose up. It was Huang, a Chinese second-year student.

I nodded towards him.

'I was just wondering, are you going to carry on your research into the electrical signals sent through the mycorrhizal networks up at Wytham Woods?'

I found myself staring at him. 'No, I'm stopping my research work.'

Huang tucked his chin in. 'Really? But the initial results were so promising, it seems crazy to stop now— Ow!' He turned and scowled at Christie, a blonde woman with ringlets sitting next to him, who'd just elbowed him in the side.

Another hand on the opposite side of the room had shot up. It was Andy, one of the students who'd been maintaining the mesh sensor network for me.

I nodded to him and felt a trickle of sweat run down my back.

'But have you had a chance to look at the data? It's fascinating. There was another huge spike in electrical activity six weeks ago. I emailed you the results, but I heard nothing back.'

Six weeks ago? I vaguely remembered the warbling alarms of the mesh sensor network when Evie had died…

The anger came out of nowhere: a white-hot express that tore through me.

'And why the hell do you think I haven't responded, Rob?'

He gaped at me as his cheeks reddened. 'Sorry, I wasn't thinking.'

'Damned right you weren't thinking. I lost my wife and my world has fallen apart since then. The last thing I've had the head-space for is stupid emails from my students.'

Andy slumped down into his chair as the other students traded shocked looks. I could feel the judgement building like static in the room.

I put my hands on either side of the lectern and glowered at them all. 'If you're all so bloody concerned about my research work, you're welcome to it. I have no interest any more.'

Huang stood up, ignoring Christie who was trying to stop him. 'But it's your life's work. You can't just throw it away like this.'

I slammed my fist on to the lectern, making it wobble. 'No, Evie was my life, my everything, my pole star in the darkness. Now she's snuffed out nothing means anything to me any more.' At some point I began crying and tears were soon streaming down my face.

This had been a mistake.

I yanked my laptop from the display connector and stuffed it and my notes into my bag. Not a single student said a thing as I rushed out through the side door, although I caught the pity in many of their faces. The moment I was outside, my eyes blinded with tears, I heard the explosion of conversation behind me. I'd just gone down in flames and my career here was as good as over.

CHAPTER 19

During the taxi ride back I'd barely registered the driver's frequent glances in the rear-view mirror as he kept half an eye on the guy having an emotional breakdown in the back of his car. Despite my best intentions to move forward again, everything had blown up spectacularly in my face.

My mind threw up a memory that fitted exactly how I was feeling.

On holiday in Cornwall, a cousin of mine had showed me the dark entrance to a mineshaft. I'd felt that abyss pulling at my feet, almost willing me to step off. Right now that was exactly how I was feeling. Was there even any point in trying to fight it? After all, what did I have left to live for?

Unaware of my internal dialogue, the taxi driver deposited me back in Wellington Square just outside my door. I paid him without making eye contact and headed up the steps towards the front door.

I was trembling so much with nervous energy that it took me three attempts to get my key into the lock. As I stepped into the hallway, Mrs Jenkins opened her door as though she'd been waiting to pounce on me. Knowing her she probably had been.

The old woman peered at me. 'You're back from work early, Adam.'

My eyes skated away from hers. 'I'm not feeling well.'

Her eyebrows drew together. 'Why, what's wrong with you?'

I cast a glance towards the stairs as a spinning sensation passed through my abdomen. 'Just not feeling great. I'm probably going down with a bad cold.'

Her features softened. 'In that case I'll make you some of my famous chicken soup. That's the perfect thing when you're feeling under the weather.'

'Honestly, you don't need to bother. A hot bath and I'll be fine.'

Mrs Jenkins shook her head. 'Nonsense! You'll have some chicken soup and that's the end of it.' She crossed her arms. 'Besides, surviving on takeaways is all well and good, but what you need in you is some proper home-cooked food.' There was warmth behind her eyes.

I had the distinct impression that we weren't just talking about chicken soup here. I could see by the determined set of her jaw that the sooner I agreed, the sooner I could get back to the safety of my flat. 'Thank you. That would be really kind of you.'

'Good.' Outside a flurry of dry leaves swirled in the porch, casting dancing shadows through the rippled glass of the door. Mrs Jenkins scowled at them. 'That will be the first sign of Abigail.'

'Abigail?' I asked.

'The hurricane that's sweeping across the Atlantic. They're telling everyone to stay indoors before it hits later tonight. They've been warning about the storm doing a lot of structural damage, even here in Oxford. You must have heard about it. It's been all over the news.'

I shook my head. 'I haven't been listening to or watching a lot of anything lately.'

She touched her lips with her fingertips and nodded.

My eyes travelled back to the staircase as the spinning sensation inside my skull increased.

'Sorry, look at me gossiping away about the weather when you need to go and lie down. I'll bring that chicken soup up when it's done.'

'Thank you,' I replied with a faint smile. With a wave I turned away and almost bolted up the stairs.

I entered my flat, closed the door behind me and leant on it, my shirt sticking to the sweat that had soaked my back. I took rapid breaths as the strength seemed to flow out of my body. I managed to make it to the sofa before I collapsed and my thoughts swirled away into oblivion.

I WOKE up to the unnatural darkness of a storm and the sound of wind groaning around the house. As my mind surfaced, I was able to focus on the kitchen clock. It was four o'clock in the afternoon. But then I noticed the day display: Friday. I'd been asleep for at least seventeen hours straight. The events of the previous day came rushing back in and a sinking feeling passed through my gut.

My head groggy, I headed to the window and looked down at the tops of trees in the park, swaying as the wind tussled their branches. At least they weren't in leaf. The coming hurricane shouldn't bring down too many branches.

As a knot of hunger tightened inside my stomach, I remembered my conversation with Mrs Jenkins. I headed to the front door and opened it a crack. Sure enough, a pot with a lid stood before my door with a note stuck through the handle. I lifted the pot up and carried it into the flat, setting it down on the worktop.

I raised the lid to see a glistening soup scented strongly with garlic and thyme. My stomach twisted tighter. Maybe Mrs Jenkins was right and home cooking was exactly what I needed. I set the soup on the stove and began to warm it on a gentle heat. Touched by her act of kindness, I pulled out the note and started to read.

Dear Adam,

Eat this up and it will help, I promise. I just wanted to say I think I know exactly what you're going through.

The smile that had started to form on my lips faded away.

You see, my Albert was stolen from me when we were only newly-weds. Like you and Evie, we never had the chance to have a child and I never knew the comfort that might have brought me. Albert died in an awful freak accident in the Cowley car factory, and it felt as if my life was over... I hope you don't mind me talking out of turn here, but I can see that same haunted look in your eyes that I had back then.

I felt a growing heaviness in my limbs as I continued to read.

I know it must seem right now that you'll never be able to get past this, Adam, and to be honest you never will, not completely at least. But day by day the pain you carry inside you will become part of who you are. Take it from someone who has been on the path that you are on now: it does eventually get easier. And believe it or not, you'll even learn to laugh again. Maybe if you're very lucky, as impossible as it feels to you today, you will love again.

The message from my heart to you, Adam, is to turn your face to life, not to the darkness. And whenever you need any chicken soup for your soul, I'm just downstairs and a door knock away.

Your friend when you need me to be,

Grace

The back of my eyes stung as I wiped away my tears. I had no idea that Mrs Jenkins's first name was Grace. She was no longer an abstract person but someone very real to me. And it sounded as if she really did understand what I was going through.

I felt profoundly moved that someone whom I'd hardly ever given the time of day to before would reach out to me with such an act of genuine kindness. In that moment I made a silent vow that I'd try to be a much better neighbour to Grace from now on.

I felt the muscles across my shoulders loosen a fraction for the first time since Evie's death. Perhaps Grace was right. If other people could survive this, maybe I could too... The question was: did I want to? My train of thought was interrupted by the buzzer sounding on the intercom.

I ignored it and lowered the temperature under the pot. The smell of it had already ratcheted up my hunger several notches.

The buzzer went again and kept going. Whomever it was pressing the button obviously meant business.

Turn your face to life... Grace had said. Maybe that journey started now. Before I could change my mind, I crossed to the intercom and pressed the button. 'Who is it?'

'It's Matt and Sarah,' Sarah's voice said, her tone strained.

At once my stomach became a hard stone ball. Here they were to have it out with me after my drunken pass at Sarah. The flicker of energy that Grace's letter had sparked fizzled out as the reality of my previous behaviour crashed back in.

I sagged into myself as I pressed the door unlock button. Time to face the music. I turned the soup off and left my flat door ajar before heading to the sofa.

I hung my head as footsteps came up the stairs and the door opened. 'Hi, guys,' I said without looking up.

Matt's feet appeared before me. I braced myself for whatever was coming, even a punch in the face. But no hands grabbed me to haul me to my feet; I heard no verbal threats, no shouts, no nothing.

My gaze travelled up his legs to see Sarah standing behind Matt as his gaze swept around the room.

I sank back into the sofa. 'Let's just get this over with.'

'Sorry?' Matt replied, his eyes widening as he looked at me for the first time rather than the shattered metaphor for my life that the flat had become.

'I know I deserve everything that's coming to me. I'm so sorry about how I behaved, Sarah.'

Matt peered at her. 'What's he on about?'

Sarah blinked rapidly at her husband. 'Nothing, Matt, apart from that Adam was spouting a whole load of nonsense the last time I was here.'

I stared at her and she shook her head the barest fraction. That was why Matt wasn't currently laying into me. Sarah hadn't told him. God, so this was what real friendship looked like. Sarah was doing her best to protect me from myself and the inevitable fallout with Matt if she'd told him the truth. Whether she'd forgive me was entirely another matter.

'Will you look at the state of you, Adam?' Matt said. 'You look like a wild man of the woods.'

'You should have seen me before I shaved,' I replied.

Matt shook his head as the wind gusted around the building and rattled the windows. 'It's going to be a big one,' he said, gazing out. 'It's made landfall in Ireland already and has done loads of damage. It will hit Oxford in full force within the next hour, so we'd better get a move on.'

I felt the tension crawling up my neck again. 'Get on with what exactly?'

Sarah put her hands on her hips. 'We're here to make an intervention.'

'What flavour of intervention?' I asked.

'One where you come and stay with us so we can look after you.'

'Jesus, don't I look like a man who can look after himself?' I said.

'Actually, mate, you really don't,' Matt replied. 'Admit it. You've totally lost the plot and don't seem to be in danger of finding it anytime soon. We both love you far too much to just stand by and let you crash and burn. So here's the deal. You go and pack the things you need in a bag and then we're taking you back to stay with us.'

Sarah nodded. 'You need to catch your breath, Adam. I've been talking to Lilly and James and we've come up with a joint plan.

We're going to help them clear most of Evie's things from the flat, apart from what you can't bear to be without. James will store everything in the attic at their place so when you're ready, you can go through them. Right now this flat feels like a mausoleum to Evie. And that's not doing you any good.' She gestured to Evie's box. 'I bet you still haven't opened that, have you?'

I shook my head. 'I just can't, not yet at least.'

'Adam, if I know anything about my sister, I'm certain she would have put her heart and soul into whatever is in there. She would have put together what's inside it to help you through this period.'

I curled my shoulders down. 'Or maybe all the love she put into the things in there will just break my heart all over again.'

'That's a big maybe, but you won't know until you open it, will you?' Matt said. 'Anyway, we can leave it here, but you're still coming with us.'

I felt the spinning sensation start up again inside me. 'No, I'm doing fine. Really.'

'Are you sure of that, Adam?' Matt said. 'And where does this "I'm doing fine" fit in with the phone call I received yesterday from Geoff?'

I laced my fingers around the back of my neck as the spinning grew faster, the wind howling outside the windows in unison. 'Geoff rang you?'

'Yes, because he was worried sick after you turned up back at work unannounced and then proceeded to have a breakdown in front of your students.'

I held up my hands to stop him. 'Okay, I admit that it was a crap idea for me to go in. I get that now.'

'Yes, maybe it was, but it was also the first tangible step to trying to get your life back to some semblance of normality,' Sarah said. 'It was just far too soon. Nobody thinks any the less of you for it. But whether you realise it or not, you need help, Adam. So you're coming to stay with us until your head is in a better place.'

'Look, guys, I appreciate the gesture. But I just need to work this through by myself.'

Sarah gestured to one of the empty whisky bottles that littered the coffee table. 'While we stand by and let you self-medicate as part of your strategy?'

'It's the only thing that's helped me so far.'

Matt shook his head. 'Exactly, Adam. You've been on a self-destructive streak for the last month. Drinking way too much, barely looking after yourself as you've tipped towards a full-blown breakdown. And we owe it to Evie to step in and save you from yourself. Don't make this harder than it needs to be.' He reached out for my arm.

I slapped his hand away. 'Stop treating me like a child, Matt!'

Sarah sighed. 'We've tried letting you get on with it and seen how that's worked out for you.' She made a sweeping gesture at the flat, ending with her pointing at the empty vodka bottles again.

'Please, just leave me alone,' I said, the tone of my voice lowering as I jammed my jaw together.

Matt shook his head. 'Not happening.' He reached out and clamped his powerful sculptor's hand around my arm. 'Come on, mate. Let's get that bag packed and leave before that storm hits.'

How could they both just stand there and tell me what to do? Hot anger surged through me as I tried to pull away from Matt, but his grip tightened like a vice and he shook his head.

'I said, fucking leave me alone!' I shoved Matt hard and he tripped on a glass tumbler I'd left on the floor. Matt fell backwards, his arms windmilling, and the back of his head slammed into the glass coffee table, shattering it into a hundred fragments. He sagged to the floor and didn't move.

Sarah and I stood rooted to the spot for a split second, staring down at him as the horror of what had happened sank in. And then a pool of dark red blood started to gather around the back of Matt's head, spreading across the wooden floor.

'Matt!' Sarah shouted. She dropped to his side, her mobile already in her hand. She punched in a number. 'Yes, I need an ambulance straight away…' she said breathlessly into it.

Her voice faded away as the howling in my mind grew to a roar.

What the fuck have I done?

I rushed past both of them and headed for the door.

'Adam, stop!' I heard Sarah say in the distance. But I was already stumbling down the stairs. I crashed through the front door into the growing wild storm winds outside.

CHAPTER 20

Already daylight was sliding into murky blackness thanks to the hurricane barrelling across the country towards Oxford. I sat on a bench hidden by a circle of trees in the middle of Wellington Square, watching my front door. Without a coat on, the chill of the winter air was seeping into my bones, but I wasn't sure if it was the cold or the adrenaline pumping through my system that was making me shake so violently.

Despite being a Friday afternoon, there weren't many people hurrying past – no one but the most determined to brave the rapidly worsening weather. The beat of the city grew slower as the storm neared and people battened down the hatches.

From my hiding place in the park I watched the ambulance scream up to the house. Curious faces peered out from the windows of the neighbouring buildings. A real-life soap opera played out before them – something to watch and later gossip about on social media. I hunched my head into my shoulders, trying to hide myself from all those judgmental eyes.

Grace, worry etched into her face, opened the door to

welcome in the paramedics, who rushed up the stairs before she'd shut it again.

A short while later, I could see the silhouettes of the people inside our attic flat, moving around like a shadow-puppet theatre.

I wished I could be curled up into a ball in my bedroom, hiding away from the latest consequences of my actions. But that sanctuary was lost to me too now. I felt like a drowning man at sea, watching his sinking yacht disappear beneath the waves, while one main thought screamed in my mind... *What if Matt dies?*

I drove my fingernails into my palms, biting down on my lip so hard that the iron taste of blood filled my mouth.

The image of Matt's head slamming into the glass table and the red pool of blood blossoming on the floor spun inside my head on an endless loop. Those awful seconds when I'd stolen away my best mate's life.

I felt numb to my core. There was no going back from this, no hitting rewind so I could do things differently. This would change the rest of my life for ever.

A movement from the front door pulled me out of the pit of my thoughts. Grace opened it and stood aside, her arms wrapped around herself. The ambulance crew rushed out, carrying Matt on a stretcher. Straight away I saw that his head had been bandaged. Sarah was right by his side, holding his hand, her face ashen as she looked down at her husband. The paramedics quickly loaded Matt into the ambulance and a moment later their vehicle sped around the square and shot away along the road, blue lights strobing.

As I watched it go, realisation hit me. Matt wasn't dead if they'd rushed him away like that. But there had been all that blood where his head had struck the coffee table. I knew enough from medical dramas that he could still die from a brain bleed. Or even if he survived, he could suffer permanent brain damage.

Grace was still at the front door, watching the road as the

ambulance disappeared. Then she caught someone staring at her from one of the windows.

She scowled at them and raised two fingers. 'Just fuck off, you nosy parker!'

At any other time I would have smiled, but not now.

Grace's eyes scanned the square as if she was looking for something and she focused on the park.

'Adam, are you in there?' she called out.

I huddled tighter into myself to make my body as small as possible, hoping the shadows were deep enough to hide me. I must have succeeded; Grace stepped back inside and closed the door with a shake of her head.

And with that simple gesture, my home, my ship, disappeared beneath the waves and I was completely alone. I dropped my head into my hands as the street lights cast dancing shadows on the floor from the swaying park trees.

'What have I done?' I whispered out loud.

'What indeed?' a man's voice replied.

I snapped my head up, but I couldn't see anyone. Stranger still, and deeply unsettling, whomever had spoken had a very similar voice to my own.

I peered into the tangle of shadows beneath a nearby beech tree. 'Is someone there?'

Two points of silver light appeared...not lights but eyes reflecting what illumination there was from the street lamps. They weren't at head height, but more as if this person was crouching on the floor.

A chill ran through my blood. 'Who are you?' I whispered.

'Surely you must recognise me?' the voice replied.

The shape moved forward into the building gloom and I gasped, my mind stuttering as the black dog emerged from the shadows.

The rational part of my brain tried to look for a logical explanation. The owner had to be just behind the beast. 'You should keep that bloody thing on a lead. It's not safe.'

The dog peered at me with far too intelligent eyes. 'You still don't understand, Adam. It's me. And I am you.'

The dog's mouth hadn't moved, yet I'd heard its words directly in my mind.

I pressed my hands to my head as though as I was trying to hold the craziness inside my skull. A sob escaped my clenched teeth. 'No…'

'Yes, Adam, and you know it's true. I'm the part of you that you tried to hide away. Your actions have unlocked me from the depths of your psyche.'

My hands clamped on to the bench. I was afraid I was going to drift up into the sky at any moment, carried away by my madness. The physical world felt as if it was shaking beneath my feet.

This couldn't be happening, couldn't be real… I began to rock backwards and forwards. 'I'm losing my mind.'

The dog chuckled, actually chuckled. I found that as disturbing as anything else.

'Or maybe you're only now finding your true sanity,' it said.

I stared at this apparition of madness, staying mute. To say anything would mean I was acknowledging that this was really happening – that I'd finally tipped over the edge.

The dog stood before me, its eyes holding mine. 'You needed someone to talk to and I'm it. So let's start looking at your situation objectively, my friend. Let's face it, you have destroyed so many bridges that there is only darkness in your future from now on. They're probably going to lock you up for what you did to Matt. And could you really live with the consequences if Matt dies from his injuries?'

I shook my head. 'No,' I croaked.

'You see, that's a rational thought right there. Then there's your breakdown yesterday, which will have convinced many that you're unfit for work. Besides, as a convicted criminal, possibly even a murderer, do you think there'll still be a job waiting for you when you're released?'

Tears beaded my eyes. 'No, they'll fire me. They'll have no choice.'

'Exactly right, Adam. And if you think there'll be any funding left for your research work after everything comes to light, you can think again.'

I stared at the dog, a manifestation of my subconscious that was making far too much sense. 'So if I conjured you up from my imagination to tell me all this, then tell me why?'

'That's a good question, Adam, but the fact you're even having this conversation means you've already descended into madness. The best you can hope for now is to be committed and so pumped full of drugs you won't even remember your own name.'

I smeared my tears away with my hand and nodded.

The dog peered deeper into my eyes. 'You've been dropped into this nightmare because you lost the woman who was your anchor in this world.'

My mouth thickened with saliva. 'So what do I do?'

The dog stood and padded towards me, muscles rippling across its powerful shoulders. In the chill air its breath steamed and I caught the rich scent of compost.

'You already know the answer, Adam,' it said. 'All you can see is pain and suffering ahead. Your hope was snuffed out when Evie died. So why continue with what amounts to a pointless struggle and extend your suffering unnecessarily?'

The wind moaned through the trees and I thought I heard someone whispering, but when I tried to tune in to it, all I could hear was the howling wind and the labouring of my own breath.

I peered into the black dog's eyes. 'You're saying I should end it?'

The dog sat down before me. 'Yes. All it takes is a moment of courage, then all your suffering will be over.'

Dry leaves scurried around my feet as the wind swirled around us. 'I don't think I can...'

'Then do this for the sake of all those who care about you – those who are being torn apart by what you're doing to yourself. It will be a mercy for them if nothing else.'

This phantom of my own being spoke with such clarity and certainty that I couldn't find an argument to counter the beast's unrelenting logic. I knew then that I'd already made the decision.

I hung my head to stare at the decaying leaves around my feet. 'Yes...' I said. A single word that would mean the end of everything.

I took a deep breath and felt a strange calmness.

The wind roared, pulling at my clothes and shaking the branches of the tree above me. The first large raindrops started to fall, hitting the ground at my feet like watery bullet fire. When I looked up again the dog wasn't anywhere to be seen. I stood up with hollowed legs and headed towards the park gate to make good on the promise I'd just made to myself.

CHAPTER 21

I'd nothing left, just an auto-pilot compulsion to reach the end of journey and get this thing done.

I leant into the wind howling between the buildings like an unleashed wild animal, placing one foot in front of the other and driving myself into the gale. Given the squalls of rain, part of my scientist's brain registered that it wouldn't be much longer before the storm hit hurricane level.

I'd no plan about how to end my life, but when I found myself in Radcliffe Square it seemed fitting to seek oblivion in the heart of Oxford where I'd had my first date with Evie.

Normally the square would have been packed out with tourists viewing the surrounding buildings that dripped with history, but now it was almost deserted. Next to me was the famous Radcliffe Camera, a beautiful neo-classical domed building. I knew the Camera part of the name had been taken from the Latin word for a large vaulted chamber. It housed part of the Bodleian Library's collection and also the reading rooms many of the students used to study.

If my subconscious had meant for me to throw myself from its roof, that wasn't going to work out. The roof was accessed through a locked door at the top and trying to get the key would raise too many questions, especially in my wild-eyed crazy-man state. No, I needed somewhere with public access. My eyes turned without my control, my subconscious serving up the answer.

I looked up at the tower of the University Church of St Mary the Virgin as pinpricks of icy rain stung my face. I was so soaked through by now that my shirt had become a glistening second skin. If I didn't kill myself soon, I would probably die of hypothermia anyway. But there was still one hurdle to get past if I wanted to use the tower. I needed access from the tearoom below it.

Head down, I followed my internal siren's call to oblivion and entered the door at the foot of the church.

A few people were huddled in the tearoom inside as the wind moaned around the building. I almost ran into a blonde woman in an apron carrying a wooden tray tucked under her arm.

'Hi, Adam.'

I stared at her and it dawned on me that this was one my students, Christie. 'Hi…'

Her gaze quickly took in my bedraggled state. She frowned, no doubt replaying her last encounter with me at college yesterday. She closed the distance between us, leaning in closer. 'Are you doing okay?'

The real answer? *No, I've destroyed my life and I'm about to throw myself from your tower.* But instead I just smiled. 'Taking it each day at a time, but getting there, Christie.'

She nodded, relief smoothing the muscles in her face. 'That's good to hear.'

I shuddered as the heat of the room alerted my body to just how frozen it had become.

Christie's gaze tightened on me. 'You really shouldn't be out in this weather, especially without a jacket. You'll freeze to death.'

My subconscious already had a lie prepared. 'I was studying at the Bodleian and got caught out. I thought I'd take shelter in here.'

'Well, you're welcome to come in and dry off, but I should warn you that I'm the last member of staff here. I'm about to call it a day and close up early because of the storm.'

'I don't blame you.' I looked past her to the stairs that led up to the tower, but I didn't want to make myself too obvious. I returned my gaze to Christie. 'I didn't know you worked here...' My voice trailed away. I couldn't exactly add, 'If I had, I might have thought of somewhere else to end it.'

'Yes, most weekends I'm here to take a small bite out of the mountain of student debt that college life has landed me with,' she replied.

'Same old...' My eyes strayed to the Do Not Enter sign on a rope across the stairs. I gestured towards it. 'I was hoping to take some photos of the storm from the tower.' The lies were coming easily now.

'Sorry, no can do – church policy and all that,' Christie said. 'It's far too windy to be safe up there.'

Oh, the irony, if only she knew it. My subconscious was already on the case and simply made a slight tweak to its plan. 'Of course, health and safety. Would you mind making me a hot drink before you close up?'

'Oh god, yes.' She grimaced and looked to the ceiling. 'I probably shouldn't be blaspheming in the vault of a church, however mildly.'

'I won't tell anyone.'

She smiled at me. 'So what do you fancy – a coffee, hot chocolate, something like that?'

'A strong black coffee would be perfect.' I patted my pocket, realising I didn't have my wallet. 'Damn! I don't have any money on me.'

Christie waved a dismissive hand. 'This will be on me. See it as my way of apologising to you for not letting you go up.'

'That's really kind of you, thanks.' I headed for a table near the roped-off entrance to the tower where I also had a clear view of Christie behind the counter.

Christie had soon deposited a steaming mug of coffee on my table, along with a slice of chocolate cake that she'd insisted was also on her. I felt a twinge of guilt at her misplaced act of kindness as I made an attempt at eating and drinking her offerings to avoid her getting suspicious.

The other patrons began to drift away, their hoods pulled up and scarves wrapped tightly around their necks, disappearing out of the door in ones and twos.

At last the moment I'd been looking for presented itself. All Christie's attention was fixed on the coffee machine she was cleaning.

Twisting my wedding ring, I stood slowly, doing my best to move in silence as I headed for the steps. With my mouth dry, I raised the rope, checking over my shoulder. Christie's attention was still on the coffee machine as she polished it while humming to herself.

I slipped under the rope and walked on the balls of my feet up the stairs into the gift shop. Inside it was situated the entrance to the tower.

As I approached the medieval stone staircase, I spotted a rat watching me with dark beady eyes. In any other situation I would have shooed it away but I found myself gazing at this overconfident creature, almost held by the spell in its gaze. I shook my head and continued on my way.

With every step up the spiral staircase, a sense of peace began to fill me. Everything about this felt right; it was the obvious answer to all my problems. I should have worked this out long before now.

I reached the top of the stairwell and had to shove the door open against the blustering wind. I stepped out on to the stone balcony and at once the stinging rain lashed into my face. I leant into the wind as if I were Prospero, having conjured up this wild tempest to mark the ending of my life.

The view from up here had been one of Evie's favourites in the city and I took a last few seconds to gaze out at it. The top of the dome of the Radcliffe Camera was opposite, the Oxford spires stretching away all around. A guy on a bicycle, head down, battled his way across the square against the weather, not spotting the crazy guy watching his progress from the church tower.

I felt something turn over inside me as my resolve hardened. The time had come.

I took a deep breath and approached the stone balustrade without so much as trembling. A sense of serenity had really taken hold now. My race was done and it was time to cross the finishing line.

Just as I placed my hand on the balustrade, metal hinges groaned from behind me. I glanced back to see Christie staring at me from the open doorway.

'Adam, you shouldn't be up here. It's far too dangerous!'

I ignored her and hopped up on to the wall. 'Don't try to stop me, Christie.'

Her hands flew to her mouth. 'What the hell do you think you are doing? Jesus, please don't do this, Adam.'

'But I have to, Christie. I have nothing left to live for.' I turned to face the precipice and opened my arms wide. *Here I am, universe, you can take me.*

'Okay, okay…' Christie replied, her tone becoming gentle. 'I can see that you're serious, but just give me ten minutes to try to change your mind.'

'There's nothing you can say,' I said without looking back at her.

'Don't you owe it to yourself to think about it for just another ten minutes? Please give me a chance to change your mind. Is that really too much to ask?'

I shrugged. 'It won't make any difference.'

'Well, you're the one holding all the cards right now. All you have to do is take one small step and leave me looking stupid. But somewhere, even if it's buried deep inside you at the moment, you have to be wondering about doing this. Apart from anything else, you need to think about all the people who care deeply about you.'

'Oh, I think I burned those particular bridges today, then blew them up with sticks of dynamite just to make sure.'

'So say you. But I for one can tell you that all your students, including me, will be devastated if you go ahead and do something so bloody stupid.'

I shook my head. 'You'd all be better off without me. And Professor Geoff Edwards is a great teacher.'

'Yes, maybe he is, but he still isn't you. Look, whether you realise it or not, this world needs people like you and the difference you can make, especially when it comes to protecting our diminishing woodlands and rainforests. In these crazy times we need genuine heroes who can capture hearts and minds. And, Adam, whether you realise it or not, you are definitely one of those great people who can help open eyes to just how incredible nature really is and why we need to look after it.' There was such a light shining in her eyes during this impassioned speech I was certain the most ardent priests who'd stood in the pulpit of the church below would be in awe of this woman.

'It almost sounds as if you actually believe that,' I said.

Christie nodded. 'Each and every one. Is there a friend who I can ring and get to talk some sense into you?'

I let out a brittle laugh. 'Not any more. I just managed to accidentally murder my best friend. I doubt his wife will want anything to do with me either.'

Christie gawped at me. 'You killed somebody?

I frowned. 'The last time I saw Matt he was being rushed to hospital in an ambulance. If he's not dead, he may at the very least have a serious head injury.'

'I see... But this was an accident?'

'Yes, but it happened after I shoved him. He fell and cracked his head open on a table.'

'Right…an accident then. And you're afraid to ring his wife to find out?'

'Why would Sarah want to have anything to do with me after what I've done? I've lost the only two people left who really cared about me.'

'Well, as I've already told you, that's absolutely not true. Every student who has taken one of your classes thinks the sun shines out of your bloody arse, to be absolutely frank.'

A laugh bubbled up from somewhere inside me. 'Good to know.'

Christie stood taller. 'And as far as this Matt and Sarah are concerned, it sounds to me as if you're making a lot of assumptions that will cost you your life unless you're prepared to challenge them. So how about this? Have you got a number for Sarah so I can find out what actually happened? I mean, what have you got to lose, Adam?'

I stared at the determined soul before me as the pouring rain soaked her blonde ringlets into a sodden mess. She, at least, really did seem to care. I felt the claws of my certainty begin to loosen their grip.

'Please, Adam, if for nobody else, do it for me. Otherwise I'll have to live with this for the rest of my life. You're too good a man to throw your life away like this.'

I hung my head. 'Too good a man… There's an irony if ever I've heard one.' I glanced up to see Christie chewing her lip. 'I guess…' I sighed. 'But you have to promise me that if it's as I thought, you're not to blame yourself for what happens next. You need to turn around and head back inside. Do we have a deal?'

She nodded. 'Yes. Thank you. So do you have Sarah's number?'

'Sorry, no mobile on me.'

'I thought you said you were going to take photos. How would you…?' Her voice trailed away and she shook her head.

'Sorry. But I can remember Matt's, though there's every likelihood he won't answer, especially if…' My throat suddenly choked up.

'Let's not go there yet, Adam. Even if he doesn't pick up, there could be dozens of reasons why.'

'Maybe…'

'So let's do this thing. What's Matt's number?'

I told Christie, who punched it into her mobile. Despite my promise, if Matt didn't pick up, I wasn't sure I would be able to stop myself taking the one small step that would result in me lying in a crumpled heap at the bottom of the tower.

Over the wailing wind, I could just hear Matt's mobile ringing at the other end of the line. It stretched on to five rings, then six, and I braced myself for the almost inevitable sound of the answer machine cutting in. But then I heard a click and a muffled woman's voice.

'Hello, my name is Christie Steward. I'm one of Adam Roberts' students. I need to talk to you urgently.' She turned away from me and walked to the far end of the balcony, bending her face to her mobile to protect it from the scudding sheets of rain. Then she nodded and headed back towards me. I couldn't quite read Christie's expression as she held out the phone.

'Sarah wants to speak to you,' she said.

I felt light-headed as I took the mobile from her and placed it to my ear.

'Adam, for god's sake don't do this.'

I stared out through the swirls of rain eddying across the square.

'Adam, I can hear you breathing. Talk to me.'

Christie gave me an encouraging look.

Bile filled my throat as I forced myself to speak. 'How is Matt doing?'

I heard a relieved sigh at the other end. 'Okay, the first thing you need to know is that Matt is going to be all right. It looked far worse than it was, although he was knocked out for a while there. We're keeping him in overnight just in case there's any brain swelling, but the signs are all positive. And even if he worsens, he's in the right place for us to move quickly enough to prevent any major problems.'

I gripped the phone tighter. 'You really think he's going to be fine?'

'I'm as certain as I can be at this stage. Look, I don't think you have any idea about how many people will be devastated if you give up like this.'

'Everybody will be better off, especially you and Matt, without me around to fuck up your lives any more.'

'No, we bloody won't!' Sarah almost shouted, loud enough to make me wince. 'We love you, and always will, whatever stupid things you do. That's the end of it.' Then she continued with a calmer voice. 'But if I can't talk some sense into you, then maybe this guy can.'

I heard a rustle at the other end of the line.

'You great idiot!' Matt replied. 'What do you think you're doing?'

'I'm so sorry, so sorry for all of it.'

'Yeah, you and me both, but it was an accident, mate. If your place wasn't such a pigsty, I wouldn't have tripped and cracked my head open. At the end of the day it was just one of those things.'

'But I thought I'd killed you…'

'Well, you'll have to try a bit harder than that if that's what you really want to do.'

Impossibly, I found myself laughing.

'Now that sound is music to my ears,' Matt said. 'So, about the rest of this nonsense, if you do this and don't succeed, I'm going to bloody kill you anyway.'

It might have been gallows humour, but it was exactly what I needed.

Matt's tone lowered. 'But seriously, mate. I know, Sarah and I both know, how tough things have been for you. If I'm honest, I blame myself for not stepping in sooner. But we're here now in any way you need us to be.'

'I know that and it does mean everything to me, but it doesn't fill the big gaping hole that Evie's death has left in my soul…' I felt clarity returning to my thoughts. 'It's a pain I can no longer live with, Matt. I hope you can understand that one day.'

'Adam—'

I hit the call end button, cutting Matt off, and handed the mobile to Christie.

She gave me a wide-eyed look. 'You can't.'

'I can. I'm really sorry, Christie.'

The mobile was buzzing in her hand as she stared at me. 'No!'

I ignored her and my senses sharpened as I took in the many spires of Oxford again, their summits piercing the scudding low clouds like dozens of swords. Then came a whispered sound, clearly audible despite the roar of the storm.

'Adam…' Evie's voice.

My toes curled inside my shoes on to the edge of the balustrade. 'You're not real!' I shouted as Christie edged towards me.

'Adam, I'm here, and I love you,' her voice said again, as if the wind itself were forming the words. I looked around and spotted a shape in the square far below. This time it wasn't a black dog but the very opposite.

A beautiful deer stood gazing up at me, the same doe I'd seen in Wytham Woods, I was certain.

'Adam, you must listen to me,' Evie's voice said in my mind.

The deer's gaze held mine and despite the swirling sheets of rain between us I felt this creature speaking to me with its eyes. And then a thought not my own appeared in my mind and I knew I had to listen to it. I turned and climbed down.

Christie dropped her arms that had been about to grab me and sagged into herself. 'Oh, thank god!'

I didn't reply and started to head past her.

She grabbed my shoulder. 'What happened? What changed your mind?'

I turned to her, blinking. 'That deer down there… I need to follow it.'

Christie wrinkled her eyes at me and glanced over the edge. 'What deer?'

I saw her gaze straight through the spot where the doe was still standing patiently, its hide beaded with thousands of tiny raindrop jewels. Poor Christie couldn't see this beautiful being that had been brought to me by this storm. I didn't answer and pushed past.

'Where are you going?' Christie called out.

I paused to glance back at her. 'Chasing a vision.'

Before she could answer, I hurried away down the stairs.

CHAPTER 22

Rain, driven by the wind, hurtled almost vertically into my face with stinging slaps as I pursued the deer through the streets of Oxford. The doe, spirit creature or whatever she was, was always just ahead of me, leading me on. She looked as solid as she had the first time I'd seen her with Evie in the woods. But I couldn't shake the feeling this creature might be another phantom conjured up by my subconscious. If so, why exactly? To counter the darkness in which I was on the brink of drowning?

I passed an empty shop doorway where a homeless guy was trying to shield himself from the driving rain and wind with layers of cardboard.

Like everyone, I passed people like this each and every day in Oxford and usually pretended they weren't really there. In my less charitable moments I'd found myself annoyed that they hadn't got themselves a job. But now, in my raw, wide-open state, I couldn't filter this guy out. His eyes caught mine and he raised his chin to acknowledge me.

I made a show of patting my pockets to imply that I had no money on me.

But the guy shook his head, dug out a black plastic bin bag and handed it to me. 'You look as if you need this more than me,' he said as he took in my soaked clothes.

My eyes prickled as I wrapped the bag around myself like a cape. 'Thank you, mate.'

'No problem.' He gestured along the street to where the doe was standing on the pavement, gazing back at me, her ears flicking in the rain. 'You'd better get a move on; it looks as if she's waiting for you.'

I stared at him. 'You can see her?'

He rubbed the side of his nose. 'Maybe I can or maybe I can't. You'll just have to work that out for yourself, Adam.'

I gaped at him as he settled himself back down within his poorly constructed shelter. Had I really just had that conversation? The bin bag was definitely draped over my shoulders, meaning that act of charity had definitely happened. I might not have thrown myself off the tower after talking with speaking dogs, but maybe I'd tipped over into a different sort of stark raving madness. Whatever this journey was, I was now committed to follow it down the rabbit hole, wherever that might lead.

I started after the doe again as she headed into Jericho, one of the more bohemian areas of Oxford. I jumped as a white van seemed to come out of nowhere, shooting past and cutting through a huge puddle. A wave of ice-cold water crashed over me, yet the van didn't even slow down. I could imagine the driver laughing to himself; I was almost certain the bastard had done it deliberately.

When I looked ahead again, a sense of heaviness filled my core. I couldn't see the deer anywhere. I hurried forward past Oxford University Press, housed in an impressive nineteenth-century building.

Where are you? Where are you?

As I raced to cross a side road, a crackle of lightning lit up the windows of the modern glass-fronted Blavatnik School of Government building on the opposite side of the road.

I'd started to cross when an instinct made me turn. The doe was waiting for me at the far end of the side road. I veered towards her as she set forward again, drawing me deeper into the labyrinth of Oxford's back streets.

The deer reached a metal bridge spanning a river about ten metres wide. This was the Thames – a river that became a large majestic version downstream, carving its way through the heart of London.

The doe slipped between the pillars and trotted over the bridge. She began walking alongside a number of narrowboats that were moored up on the river.

As I followed, the shadows grew darker under the thrashing trees overhead. Curls of smoke drifted up from the silver and black chimneys of the boats, the stoves inside working overtime against the storm's chill that sought out the cracks in the boats' armours.

The wind was already whipping up waves from what was normally a perfectly calm surface. The boats' hulls slapped against the embankment as the clouds continued to flicker with lightning.

I continued behind the deer, who kept stopping for me whenever I fell too far back, drawing me onwards along the path. But I already had a strong instinct about where we were headed. There couldn't really be any doubt; following the Thames was almost a direct route to Wytham Woods several kilometres outside town. We were going to the one place I'd been avoiding. But one of Evie's pet phrases had been to lean into your fear. That was exactly what I needed to do right now if I was going to see this thing through.

I fell into my stride as I followed the deer out on to the wide-open expanse of Port Meadow. The outlines of horses hunkered down were just visible around me through the sheets of lancing rain, like large rocky mounds. With no trees or buildings to shelter me from the claws of the storm, the wind buffeted and attacked me. I angled my body into it, fighting for every step.

The light of the city was falling behind me now, the world reduced to abstract smudges in the charcoal darkness. Another boom of thunder straight overhead shook the ground and a shaft of broken light crackled into one of the trees bordering the meadow. The flash blinded me for a moment and when it cleared I couldn't see the doe anywhere.

I stood frozen to the spot as another flash of lightning crackled through the sky, illuminating the rising hill of Wytham Woods ahead of me. Another kilometre or so and I would be standing within the cover of the trees.

I set forward again, driving one foot in front of the other as the wind snarled around me. I kept to the edge of the river, the only landmark that I could now make out within the strengthening hurricane, a gurgling, frothing mass of swollen storm water.

The minutes became twenty as I crawled towards the far end of the meadow. As I passed a large willow tree whipping around in the storm, goosebumps prickled across my skin. Before I even turned around, I already knew that the black dog was back.

'Adam, it's not too late,' the beast said with my own voice as it padded towards me.

'Leave me alone,' I hissed.

'How can I when I'm part of you? I'm the despair that is constantly lapping around your heels, the thing that steals your hope. I'm the part of you that's being realistic and showing you things for what they are.'

I didn't reply. I knew, whatever I said, that this thing would twist my words and use them against me. After all, it already knew all the arguments I had to counter it.

The dog's eyes flickered in the storm, locking on to mine. 'There are some heavy stones on the bank just over there. You could load them into your pockets to weigh yourself down and then jump into the river. Then all the anguish about losing Evie would be over, because, let's face it, Adam, you're never going to get over losing her.'

'No, I won't!' I shouted. I hauled my eyes away from the thing's hypnotising grip and started forward again. But behind me I could hear the dog continuing to track me through the roar of the storm.

'I heard what Sarah said to you, but do you honestly think that changes anything?' the dog said. 'They're just words after all. They can't change what's happened.'

I quickened my step, wanting to get away from the darkness of my own psyche trying to wear me down.

My boots splashed through the growing puddles as the water began to rise and lap the banks of the Thames. Soon it would seek out the flood plain of Port Meadow and attempt to turn it into an inland sea.

'Adam, you can't get away from yourself, so why even try?' the beast whispered directly into my mind.

'Because I don't need or want you.'

The dog laughed with my own laugh. 'Good luck with that. You might as well try cutting off your own head. You see, I'm woven into the darkness between your atoms; I'm that sense of hopelessness that lies at the heart of every human being. And like so many others caught in that web, there is no point to your existence any more. End this, Adam, and end it now. The water is so swollen I don't think you'll even need stones now.'

'I said, leave me fucking alone!' I screamed. I burst into a run and vaulted over a fence. Just ahead was a grey-stone building next to the roaring water of a weir that cut across the Thames. This was a pub I'd eaten at with Evie in another life, its windows now dark, having obviously shut early.

The Thames roared over the weir, a thunder of water sending plumes of spray over the building. I raced to a gate at the far end but found it locked and too high to scale. I doubled back to a small wooden footbridge that had been left to rot for years. It vibrated as the water thundered around its supports. I started to sprint across, feeling the boards shaking beneath my feet. But then I skidded to a stop – the dog had somehow got there before me and was now blocking my way off the bridge.

'Look, this is the perfect opportunity, Adam. You really won't have long to suffer.'

'Fuck off!' I lowered my head and charged towards the creature. But as I braced myself to crash into the dog, it broke apart like smoke before reforming behind me.

I was on the opposite bank and racing along the path up to the old stone road bridge beyond the pub. Without looking back I shoved open the gate and ran out on to a road.

With a screech of brakes, an SUV skidded to a stop, blaring its horn. I crashed through the opposite gate and sprinted down the slope back towards the Thames. Ahead of me, now shrouded by shimmering curtains of rain, Wytham Woods were less than a kilometre away.

I was running faster than I ever had in my life, but still I heard the heavy slap of paws behind me.

'Adam, there is no hope, there is nothing, just the oblivion that sucks at your thoughts and steals everything away that you love,' the beast murmured in my mind like a parent telling their child an unpleasant truth.

'I won't listen to you any more!' I shouted.

The wind bellowed and a large willow tree ahead splintered as if it had been hit with cannon fire, toppling into the wild waters of the rushing Thames.

I ignored it all, my feet thundering through the puddles and sending water flying.

The woods were a few hundred metres away across the field to my left. I veered away from the Thames straight towards them. The wind snarled and whipped away my bin-bag cape and threw it into the night. Then the black beast was streaking alongside me, a hell hound matching me stride for stride.

'You're going to die tonight, Adam. You'll be extinguished, snuffed out like a candle flame.'

A sob rattled my throat. It was right: how could I get away from myself?

The perimeter fence of the woods was less than a hundred metres away. But lactic acid was burning through my muscles. I gritted my teeth as rain lanced into my face, sapping away the last of my energy.

My foot fell into a hole hidden by a large puddle, and I sprawled on to the mud face first. Pain twisted through my ankle as I clutched my sides, heaving in lungfuls of air, dribble trailing from my mouth into the black water. I rolled over to see the dog standing over me, silhouetted against the scudding storm clouds like a tear in the world. I felt so tired and alone. I had nothing left.

The dog lowered its face to mine. 'You know you can drown in just a few centimetres of water, Adam. All you need to do is turn over and press your face into that puddle.'

A cry broke my lips as hammering blows of rain struck my chest. I'd nothing left to argue with. To die would be to find peace at last. Like an obedient child, I rolled over and pressed my face into the freezing water.

As I swallowed, hot pincers gripped my heart. At once a wild animal instinct to survive kicked in and I began to push myself up on my arms. But then I felt a massive pressure on my back, pinning me down into the water.

'Easy, Adam, don't fight it. Just give in now,' the dog whispered as its paws ground me into the freezing puddle.

Despair swept through me as the water flooded my mouth again.

He'd won.

But then a rising melody of notes reached my ears, faint but crystal clear despite the scream of the hurricane. In that moment of darkness the music punctured me, changing me, changing the flow of the energy seeping away from me into the beast of despair. As if a switch had been thrown, I felt fresh determination rush through me.

No, not this, never. I don't choose this. I choose life.

And then the weight on my back was gone as if it had never been there and I was pushing myself up on my arms.

My eyes darted in every direction. The dog was gone. But the music wasn't. It still drifted through the trees towards me, a thread of hope within the howling wind. My heart rose at the touch of Evie's song, my heart beating stronger. And there on the other side of the fence at the edge of the woods I saw the doe waiting for me again.

I stood, my fear vanquished, and headed after her. With every stride, the notes grew stronger, wrapping their spell around me.

The deer dipped her head, turned and slowly walked away into the woods. I clambered over the tall fence to follow, ignoring the sting of the barbed wire as it punctured my palms. On the other side, I headed into the woods as the wind that had lost its prey snarled at my back.

CHAPTER 23

The trees thrashed around above me as the wind roared and growled like a monster in its pursuit of me. But I was barely aware of it as I followed the deer deeper into the woods and the music gradually faded away like someone was turning down the volume. I was only another hundred metres in when the whistling sound of the wind fell silent too as every branch around me stilled. Overhead the bare winter trees were silhouetted against a star-filled sky containing a slither of a crescent moon more vivid than anything I'd ever seen over Oxford before.

The storm had vanished as if it had never been.

I turned around to see that the trees at the edge of the woods were still shaking, the scudding clouds visible in the distance. Yet within the boundary of the woods everything was still; a three-kilometre-wide circle of clear air hung over it. It was as though an invisible force field had been raised around the woods. As if things couldn't get any more surreal, I noticed I was rapidly warming up and had even stopped shaking. Despite being soaked through just a moment ago, when I ran my fingers over the cloth of my shirt it was now bone-dry.

Thoughts crashed around in my head at this sudden impossible change of my reality. How could this be?

Then a whisper came from the woods ahead of me. 'Adam...' Evie's voice.

My scalp tingling, I stopped. I ignored the rational voice inside my brain telling me this couldn't be true and I called out, 'Evie, is that really you?'

There was no reply.

Okay, so even if I was having a total mental breakdown, did it really matter if I got to see even a phantom version of my wife? No – I'd happily trade the final vestiges of my sanity for a few seconds with her, even it was only to say goodbye.

The doe waited just ahead, watching me with her big, quiet eyes.

'Okay, spirit guide, or whatever you are, let's see where this journey you're leading me on ends up.'

The deer dipped her head as though she'd understood and set off again between the trees.

Soon we reached a slope and climbed upwards, the doe moving in almost complete silence. The gentle sigh of her breathing and my footfalls were the only sound in the woods now.

I followed the deer and the sense of peace radiating from the trees reached into me.

But then a chilling thought struck me. Maybe there *was* a rational explanation for all this. What if I'd actually thrown myself off that tower after all – and everything that had happened since was a construct of my dying mind? Could it be that what had seemed like an hour since I'd left St Mary's was actually just the milliseconds it took for my consciousness to flow away from my broken body? All of this could have been my own personalised version of a tunnel of light.

I smiled to myself. It was as good an explanation as any. In any case, my subconscious, if that was what this was, then decided to really up its game.

As I followed the deer, my eyes gradually grew accustomed to the darkness beneath the trees, which was punctuated by shafts of white light. When I glanced up, the crescent moon was no longer; it was now full. I shook my head with wonder but accepted that too.

We reached Arwen, as I instinctively knew we would, and the tree was bathed in silver moonlight. I let out a gasp as a shape moved out of the shadows beneath it and stepped towards me.

No, not the black dog. Not here, not now.

But then the dappled light caught the curls of a silver beard and greying hair.

Silva raised his hand to greet me. 'I wondered when you would arrive, Adam.'

The doe walked straight up to him and nuzzled his hand. It was as unexpected as it was beautiful.

I could almost feel a tangible connection between this wild animal and the old man.

The doe moved away a short distance and then turned to watch us both. I approached Silva, who held out his hand.

I shook it as I asked, 'Is this a dream?'

Silva laughed and clasped my hand in both of his. 'Now there's a question.'

'And the answer is?'

'I'll answer that with my own question. What is a dream, Adam?'

'The random noise of your subconscious.'

'Maybe, but isn't it also when the constraints of your physical world fall away as your mind is set free? And here's the thing, Adam. In the everyday waking world, people lock themselves away in mental prisons.'

I peered at the old man. 'I'm not sure I follow?'

'Have you heard of the observer effect?' Silva asked.

'Yes – it's something Matt loves to discuss into the small hours when he's had one drink too many.'

'And how does he explain it?'

'He says it's what we've learned from quantum mechanics. Our particle reality comes into existence when the waveform version of it collapses. Matt says we literally create the world around us by experiencing it.'

Silva nodded. 'And Matt is quite right. If you extrapolate that thought, the way you feel has a tangible effect on it too. Look at your own recent experiences, Adam. While Evie was still alive, your world seemed full of light. But now she's gone, that same world seems filled with shadows and despair, despite it being the very same.'

'Of course it does. I've been out of my mind with grief! I don't quite see what you're driving at here.'

Silva ran his fingers through his beard. 'Your reaction demonstrates part of the reason why it's hard for people to ever see what's truly going on. Your reality is not necessarily the reality that someone else inhabits. Christie and the homeless man you encountered on the way here exist in a different world to the one that you experienced today.'

'How do you know about them?' I said, as I watched the doe bend its head to nibble at some bracken.

'Maybe it's easiest to think of this in terms of the theme of your wedding.'

'*A Midsummer Night's Dream,* you mean?'

'Exactly, albeit in the middle of winter,' Silva replied, his smile widening. 'The point is that there is so much more going on beyond what even you can see, Adam, just as in the play.' He crouched down and pointed to the dead leaves lining the ground. 'To start with, each death is part of the cycle of life on this world. It always has been.' He stuck his hand into the soft soil and pulled up a handful of dirt threaded with white lines. 'What am I holding here?'

'The rich woodland loam. It's full of minerals and nutrients, thanks to the decomposing leaves that form the majority of the soil in Wytham. And those white threads running through it are the fungal mycelium that form the mycorrhizal network.'

'Exactly. And from the death of the leaves flourishes this new life just beneath the surface.' He stood and pointed to my chest. 'All the heavy elements of this world woven into your own body were created in the heart of a supernova when a star died. Those massive explosions flung material out into the cosmos that ultimately led to life. And all creatures on this planet are children of the stars. This is the endless dance of life, all beings living their lives that are one day ended so that other new beginnings can come after them. Things have always come and gone in this eternal cycle. It's just the unbreakable law of the universe.'

'That may be true, but it's also the same mechanism that has stolen my soulmate away. Evie was the spark that made everything possible. Now she's gone, I simply can't live without her.' I hung my head.

Silva squeezed my shoulder. 'And that's a huge part of the struggle of what it is to be human. You are blessed with self-awareness and a sense of your own mortality, and those you love. So here is a hypothetical question for you, Adam. Would you rather have not met Evie in the first place and therefore be spared the pain of her loss?'

'Of course not.'

'Precisely. This is the flip side of opening your heart to someone: you leave yourself exposed in the event that they will die before you. But here's the thing. You have fallen into a common trap where you're focusing on Evie's death rather than celebrating her life. You should cherish the living memory of her that remains within you and continue to live in such a way so that you can honour her memory. You see, she has never really gone away and will always be with you in spirit. Rather than grieve for her loss, be grateful for the time you had together and the opportunity you had to learn from someone who was truly an exceptional soul.'

I ran my fingers over the trunk of Arwen as I gathered my thoughts. 'I'm obviously grateful for everything that we had and that such an incredible woman chose me to be with. But a memory can't hug me close, or hold my hand while I walk in the park. I can't share a wonderful meal or watch crap TV with a memory, nor make love to it. How can I continue to exist with the soul-crushing pain of her loss?'

The corners of Silva's mouth turned down. 'I'm afraid you can't escape it, not completely. The grief you're feeling is part of humanity's gift of being mortal. And Evie dying at such a young age is a very painful reminder that life can be far too short sometimes.'

'We were meant to grow old together, Silva, that was our plan.'

'And now your happy ever after has been stolen away. This is where I need to be totally honest with you. Your old life, the one you had with Evie, the old you – none of those things you'll ever get back to. And that pain you're feeling is never going to go away completely. But believe it or not, that's okay too. It might not feel like it from where you are standing right now, because so far all you've been able to see is darkness ahead. But, Adam, you're also becoming stronger than you've ever been in your life. You're going to be capable of doing things you could only have dreamt of before now.'

I shook my head. 'I'm not sure I share your optimistic view. I hate the person I've become: someone who wallows in his own grief, pushing everyone he loves away and lashing out at those who care. If I were my friend, I'd have given up on myself as a lost cause.'

Silva sighed. 'Adam, nobody expects you to be perfect, especially when everything is so painful. Without wanting to sound trite, it's actually these moments that truly build who people are. Everyone is an intricate, complicated and beautiful tangled web of experiences. What you've been going through since Evie's death would be true for nearly anyone who's experienced something similar. Yes, you may not have measured up to your own standards of what it is to be a decent human being, but you are also being far too hard on yourself. Don't be ashamed of this time. It's all part of your healing process. Ultimately, when you're feeling ready, you can take a risk to embrace life and get out there again. Take a chance and you'll eventually find peace.'

I watched an iridescent green rose chafer beetle scurrying through the leaf mould and up on to Silva's foot. 'You really think I can?'

'I know you can, Adam,' Silva replied.

I watched the beetle, mesmerised as it ran up his leg. 'You need to see what can be possible rather than what's been, however cherished those memories are. Don't be distracted by the shadows thrown up by your mind, especially at a time like now. Sometimes even to live takes an act of courage...and you have more courage inside you than you know.'

I raised my shoulders. 'You make it all sound so easy.'

The beetle clambered up to the old man's chest, drawing my gaze back to Silva's face. 'Oh, I'm not saying it will be easy, but it will get *easier*, that I can promise you. Gradually the hole that exists in the centre of your being that was left by Evie's death will fill as a love for life begins to tip inside to fill that void. Of course, that scar will never heal completely, but over time it will become part of who you are.'

'But I still keep coming back to why I should even try, Silva?'

'Because life is such a precious gift that you mustn't simply just throw away. Besides, the world you live in is a troubled one, maybe more troubled than it's ever been. The disconnect between people and the natural world has never been greater. Earth is being slowly killed by humanity's actions that have accelerated global warming. Your world needs champions to open the eyes of the many who refuse to see the consequences of their short-term actions.'

'And how can I help that process? I'm just one guy who studies trees for a living.'

'Because what you have been learning here in this woodland really matters, Adam, as Christie told you. It's not only trees that have their own invisible networks binding them together; people do too. Humanity far too often sees itself as something separate from nature, sometimes even its master instead, rather than being intrinsically linked to it.'

The beetle settled on Silva's shoulder and appeared to be looking directly at me along with him, which seemed almost normal to me in this incredible situation.

'All life, Adam, has an interconnected network, just like the trees that your research has helped reveal. You are going to be part of a revolution that will impact human thinking for ever – when people realise they are actually joined together too.'

'People are part of a network...' My voice trailed away as the idea filled my mind with endless possibilities. 'That humans might have their own sort of mycorrhizal network is quite a profound thought. God, Evie would have loved to talk about all this.'

'Oh, I promise you, she already knows, Adam...or, I should say, she now remembers the true nature of the world that she existed within.'

My heart caught as I thought of the music I'd heard when I'd entered the woods. 'You're talking about her in the current tense, as if she's here.'

'Evie's always been here, Adam. She is a whisper among the trees.'

Silva turned towards the doe that was once more watching us. She began to glow with golden light. As her aura intensified, static washed over my skin and I had to shield my eyes from the now blinding light.

'What's going on?' I asked.

When there was no response, I turned to Silva, but he was nowhere to be seen.

Light beams lanced out from the deer as something incredible began to happen, meaning that I – my world, my future – would be changed for ever.

CHAPTER 24

The trees started to rustle, although no wind brushed my face. Slowly a pattern emerged from the rhythmic scratching of the branches and I quickly recognised the haunting notes of Evie's song again. Then sparkles of light appeared, hovering like small stars around me. The points of light grew more brilliant as the music began to come from everywhere.

I hooked my hands around the back of my neck, slowly turning. Joy bubbled up through me and I whooped. This was beyond beautiful: a poem of light and sound carved from the air.

But my logical scientist's instinct was still ticking over. There had to be a source for this sound. It seemed to have originated with the rustling of the trees so...

I reached out and placed my hand on Arwen's trunk. The surface buzzed under my palm. To confirm my theory, I headed over to one of the neighbouring beech trees. Sure enough, when I touched it, it was vibrating too. I laughed at the sheer wonder of it.

The trees were performing Evie's music as instruments of an orchestra. Unlike last time – when I'd simply detected them reacting to her music – now they were the actual source.

The song swirled around me, growing stronger. Then faint tendrils of light began to run across every surface of the woodland floor, a spiderweb of luminance connecting to the trees.

I laughed, moving my hands to the top of my head as I drank in the strengthening spectacle. I knew exactly what this was; something I'd previously only seen modelled on a computer screen. This was the mycorrhizal network that normally lay hidden beneath Wytham Woods.

I felt light-headed, almost weightless, as the deer walked up to me over the floor of threaded gold. I reached out my hand and the deer nuzzled into it. Her coarse fur and cool nose were very much real beneath my touch. I gazed into the doe's eyes as the pulsing light grew stronger around us.

Millions of lines converged on Arwen, the central hub in this network of light. The pinprick stars drifted around her like luminous pollen, dancing and spiralling in time to the swelling music. Then they started to coalesce, forming an abstract shape. I blinked back tears as a woman formed from light began to appear.

I slowly put out a hand and the points of light rippled around my fingers. I stared at the phantom before me, barely daring to say anything in case it broke this perfect spell.

'Evie, is that really you?' I whispered.

The apparition smiled. As her mouth moved, her voice came from all around me, a vibration from the trees. 'Yes, Adam.'

I cupped my hands over my mouth as I stifled a sob and nodded.

Evie pointed to a fallen tree. 'Let's sit for a moment, Adam.'

The light particles of her form broke apart briefly, flowing through the air to knot themselves back into Evie sitting on the tree bough.

I sat next to her. All I could do was just stare at this being of pure light. A million emotions crowded my thoughts, but in the end there was only one I wanted to say.

'I love you so much, Evie,' I whispered softly.

'I love you too, for ever and a day,' she replied.

I had a desperate urge to hold her, but how can you hold a shimmer of light hanging in the air?

'I don't understand how you can be here. None of this can be real, can it?' I asked.

She laughed. 'Oh, Adam, you so always need to put something in a box to try to understand it. But to answer your question, yes, I'm really here and, no, you're not hallucinating.'

My mind scrambled as I tried to make sense of it. 'So you're telling me that part of you is still alive in here?'

'Not in the sense that you mean. I no longer have a physical body. However an echo of me still exists within these woods, just as Silva told you.'

I blinked rapidly. 'I'm still not sure that I understand…'

'Think of it like this. Part of me exists here like ripples in a pond, long after the stone that caused them has disappeared beneath the surface.'

'So you're a ghost then?'

'No – here I am in the trees, the woods, the birds, the insects, even the rat you saw in St Mary's.'

'And the deer that brought me here?'

'Yes, that was me too. You see, even though you didn't realise it, I have always been around keeping an eye on you – along with Silva.'

I slowly nodded and reached out to try to touch her, but my hand brushed through her face with little tingles of static. 'God, I've missed you so much, Evie.'

Her mouth turned down. 'I know you have, Adam. And if I could take that pain away, I would in a heartbeat. But that is the way life is. Love and sorrow, joy and pain, all woven together. You can rarely have one without the other.' She gestured towards my heart. 'But one day that broken part of you will begin to heal.'

'You really believe that?'

'I know it, but the key thing is, you must make it your truth as well, for we become what we believe.'

I gazed out among the trees. 'That sounds like good advice, but despite everything you've told me, the simplest explanation is that I've gone insane. After all, the evidence is pretty much stacked towards that conclusion.'

Evie laughed. 'I get that. Your mental equation probably runs like this: emotional trauma plus seeing weird shit equals "I'm losing my mind". Is that about right?'

I smiled. 'Pretty much.'

'Well, how about this for a replacement equation? Emotional trauma plus seeing weird shit equals "my mind has been opened up to something that people have forgotten". I know Silva has already told you that woodland myths and legends were very real to people in times long ago. But has it ever occurred to you that our ancestors might have been closer to the truth than we are today?'

'Oh, come on, Evie. You're talking to a scientist. I have a natural aversion to believing in fairy stories.'

'Says the man who is currently talking to his dead wife in what basically amounts to an enchanted forest.'

I laughed then, a real laugh – the sort that Evie could always coax from me however foul my mood. God, it felt great talking to her. The best sort of healing.

'Okay, I take your point,' I replied.

'That's more like it. So try thinking of it this way,' Evie said. 'Rather than this all being a trick of your mind, what if it's our reality that's the illusion?'

'Are you saying our world isn't actually real?'

'Not quite that, but maybe really more like an echo of something even more wonderful that exists just beyond our human senses. A higher reality, if you want to call it that. And what you've been seeing, rather than being some sort of illusion, could be viewed as a gift; the blinkers have been taken from your eyes and you're seeing things as they truly are.'

I held up my hands. 'Please stop. This is starting to make my head ache.'

Her ghostly apparition snorted, the sound coming from dozens of trees. 'Oh, my perfect idiot, all right. But you understand what I'm trying to tell you?'

'Okay, let me give this my best shot. You're saying that you're the one dreaming me?'

'That's as good a description as any,' Evie replied with a wide smile.

'So can you explain the hell hound that's been stalking me?'

'I'm afraid that creature was created from your own darkness, Adam – a reflection of the internal battle raging inside you. Your pain, your anguish and your anger formed it. But that dog also served its purpose: to help you wake up at the final moment when you faced your own oblivion. With every argument that you used to counter it, every time you didn't give in, you found another reason to live.'

'Yes…' I breathed in the scent of the woods and thought I could possibly smell a hint of vanilla within it. I gazed into my soulmate's eyes. 'Evie, I've felt so lost without you.'

'I know, Adam, and that's why you need to open the box I left for you. I knew you would probably fall apart after I was gone – I would have been exactly the same if it had been the other way around. So I filled up that box with things that will help you in your journey ahead.'

'But it's hard to believe that anything good will ever happen again after this.'

'No, there you're wrong. Remember what Silva told you about how your emotions create your own version of reality. He was absolutely right about that. When you change the filter through which you see the world, everything can change in a heartbeat. So when I'm gone, I want you to open the box and see what treasures I've left for you. I promise they will help.'

Adrenaline surged through me. If I could have, I would have clung on to Evie's apparition so she couldn't go. 'Please don't leave me alone again, Evie.'

Her sigh echoed between the trees. 'You still don't understand, Adam. I'll never leave you. A fragment of my own soul is lodged in your heart and you'll always carry that part of me with you as a living, breathing memory. Love never dies. Look for other fragments of who I was around you, and you'll find they're everywhere. Visit the places that we loved and I'll be there. I'll always be that whisper on the wind speaking into your soul, reminding you just how beautiful life is. You have so much love inside you that you can share with the world to make it a better place. And one day, when you're ready, maybe you'll find yourself opening up to loving somebody else again.'

My eyes sparkled with tears. 'I can never see that happening.'

'Maybe not now, but, as the saying goes, time really is a great healer. Don't shut yourself away from the idea, because who knows what magic may be waiting for you in your future. Live your life with an open heart, Adam, and that is the best tribute you could ever give my memory. And always know how much I love you.'

I nodded, sending my tears rolling down my cheeks. 'And me you, always.'

'Exactly, and our song will continue until the end of time,' Evie said. She reached out and brushed my face with a hand and I felt a surge of joyous energy at her spectral touch. The pure emotion was all-consuming and my tears became ones of joy. But then my heart lurched; Evie was disappearing as the particles making her up began to evaporate.

'Farewell, Adam, for now…' her voice whispered as she vanished completely and the music faded away among the trees.

I stared into the empty air where she'd been a second ago, but my grief didn't flood back in, because I could still feel her presence in the woods around me. I could even still smell her scent of vanilla too.

A red underwing moth fluttered by and landed on something at the base of Arwen. I crossed to it and gasped. It was standing on Evie's box, yet the last time I'd seen it, it had been in the flat. I knelt before the box as the moth flew away. My hands trembling, I unhooked the catch and raised the lid.

On top was a printed photo book. I began to go through the pages, smiling and crying at the many magical moments Evie had chosen for this compilation of memories.

Below the book were twelve sealed letters, one for each month starting in January the following year. Under that were other items too, including a pebble I remembered Evie picking up on a Cornish beach and presenting to me as a wishing stone, telling me that by carrying it we would win the lottery the next week. We didn't, of course. There were more items like that – things that would mean nothing to anyone else but everything to me. There were even recipes of my favourite dishes that she'd cooked for me and printouts of holiday destinations that we'd said we would always visit, including the Northern Lights in Iceland. We'd never managed it, but a label was stuck to them, saying it was up to me now to live the dream for both of us.

At last I reached the bottom and pulled out some rolled papers tied with an emerald ribbon. I undid it and gazed at the music sheets in my hand. At the top of the first page Evie had finally given her composition a name, *Silvanus*. With that the last part of the puzzle fell into place and I finally understood everything. At last I knew who the old man really was.

'Just perfect, Evie,' I whispered.

The trees rustled once again and I heard her music drifting between the boughs from a faraway place.

In that moment I knew that Evie would always be alive

through her music. Whenever I heard it I would hear her; it would be a living echo of her beautiful soul.

I clutched the sheets to my chest and wept as I felt a weight being lifted from me and the emptiness inside my chest closed up a fraction.

As golden light crept across the sky overhead, birdsong began to call out around me, a thousand voices raised to greet the light of a new day.

CHAPTER 25

I sat in the car, with Evie's box cradled on my lap. This was the day that all the preparations had been building towards for the last few weeks. Numerous cars were already parked up around the old lodge house in Wytham Woods, among them several large minibuses of the Oxford Symphony Orchestra, their logo emblazoned on the sides. It had been a major logistical operation getting their instruments up here, but Geoff had stepped in to help, along with the whole team responsible for managing Wytham. Soon, a miracle of organisation had been well under way.

I ran my fingers over the dips of the carvings of the box that contained Evie's treasures. The most precious was her *Silvanus Symphony*, which I'd handed over to the conductor of the Oxford Symphony Orchestra a month ago. Callum had personally reassured me that he and the orchestra would do full justice to Evie's music today. I'd deliberately stayed away from their rehearsals as I didn't want to spoil the surprise. I wanted to hear it with fresh ears on this most important of days.

I looked closer at the box and for the first time noticed the creatures carved among the branches. There was a mouse, a rook, and smaller birds such as robins and blue tits. There was even a red kite soaring near a crescent moon. At the base of the large tree were more creatures: a mouse, a beetle, a rat and a rabbit. Then I noticed the two deer in the distances: a stag and a doe.

A lump filled my throat. How had Evie known about all these spirit creatures when she'd commissioned this box from Matt? Was it yet another example of the magic that had been woven around me?

After that mysterious night, everything had changed for me, a fundamental realignment of how I now saw the world. I would never go back to my blinkered view of reality. Perhaps more importantly, the darkness that had been sucking at my soul had begun to dissipate and I hadn't seen the black dog again...not that I expected to. Its role in the play of my life was done. In its own way it had even helped me – to choose life over oblivion. Evie and Silva had been right about how I would begin to heal. Gradually I started to live again, to allow myself to have hope about the future.

I often thought back to when I'd seen Evie in the woods. The one thing I knew for certain was that it hadn't been a dream, not least because her box had been magically transported to the woods. Magic might have been a strong word, especially coming from a scientist, but I'd no choice but to come around to that incredible idea.

There was more recent evidence too.

I'd been back to the woods many, many times, and I could still feel Evie's presence there; I could catch her scent sometimes on the breeze. If I strained my ears hard enough, I often thought I could even hear her whispering my name.

I ran my fingers over the much-loved box. I'd dipped into it on a daily basis for the last three months. At the beginning, Evie's choreographed collections of photos, mementos and love letters had left me in tears. But gradually those tears had become ones of gratitude rather than loss. More recently, the tears had passed and examining the contents of that box now lifted me up just as Evie had always intended.

A rap of knuckles on the car window nearly made me jump out of my skin.

'Hey, Adam, is the guest of honour coming or not?' Matt said, standing next to the car. He was wearing a suit that looked a size too small. Sarah stood next to him in a pretty floral dress. She smiled encouragingly at me.

I patted the box and placed it down on the passenger seat before opening the door.

'I can't believe it's Evie's memorial at last,' Sarah said as I got out and she kissed me on the cheek.

'Me neither,' I replied. 'I know we've been preparing for it for a while, but it still seems to have sneaked up on us.'

'I guess that's the way of these things: everyone gets so caught up in the preparations that it's almost a surprise when the big day eventually comes. Anyway, we'd better get up there – unless we want the memorial to start without us.'

I walked between Sarah and Matt, our arms looped through each other's, and we headed up the track that was thankfully dry, spring weather finally arriving after loads of rain. In front of us the last knots of people were disappearing into the woods, all following a path that had been marked out with red ribbons.

Matt gave me an anxious sideways look. 'Adam, I hope you like what I've done.'

'Mate, will you please relax? I know that whatever you've created is going to be great.'

Sarah nodded. 'As always, my husband is being way too modest. But you know that he always gets like this before an opening. He doesn't need to worry – this piece really is beautiful, maybe his best work yet. I know Evie would have loved it.'

'In that case, I'm looking forward to seeing it more than ever.'

Ahead of us, voices grew louder. It seemed as if hundreds of people had gathered in the woods for Evie's memorial, from close friends to the great and the good of Oxford. We navigated our way through the crowd, exchanging hugs, kisses and handshakes. Lilly and James gave us a cheery wave from the middle of a group of people they'd been talking to.

To one side of the gathering the orchestra were already seated on the chairs that had been set up for them under the woodland's new spring canopy of leaves. On stands in front of each of the musicians was the sheet music for Evie's symphony.

People had gathered around a cloth-covered object about three metres tall. Matt hurried over to it and peeked beneath the material.

Sarah sighed. 'Matt feels he needs to do justice to Evie's memory and he's worried sick that he's going to fall short. He's also desperately concerned with what you'll think of it.'

'It could be a pile of logs and I would still find something beautiful in it.'

'Oh, I promise you it's so much more than that,' Sarah said with a smile.

She took hold of my hand and towed me towards a trestle table where a couple of my students were giving out flutes of champagne and orange juice to the crowd.

It was only as we approached that I realised that Christie, her blonde curls tamed with a band, was one of the two volunteers.

'Hey, you,' she said.

'Hey, yourself,' I replied. I turned to Sarah, passing her a champagne flute and taking a glass of orange for myself. 'Can you give me a moment? I just need to catch up with my student.'

'Sure,' Sarah said, her gaze lingering on Christie.

I shook my head at her. 'It's nothing like that.'

She grinned at me and headed towards Matt who was pacing around the covered object like a caged animal.

'Can I have a word in private, Christie?' I said.

'Of course.' She nodded to the guy helping her and then followed me a short distance away from the gathered crowd.

I looked at my glass and tapped my fingers against it before I raised my eyes to hers. 'Look, I wanted to thank you for what you did that night. If it wasn't for you, I doubt I'd be standing here right now.'

'I'm just glad I was there when you needed someone to talk to. We all hit rock bottom at some point and that's when talking to other people can really help.'

'You sound as if you speak from experience?'

Christie's lips thinned and she nodded. 'Yes.'

I noticed a robin watching us and smiled to myself. 'So how come you're so good at counselling?'

Her face fell. 'I lost a boyfriend in my first year of college. He took his own life with an overdose.'

'Shit, I'm so sorry. I didn't know.'

'Don't be. You had no way of knowing. I kept it to myself and ended up in a pretty dark place because of that. A college counsellor helped me through the harder days. And that's why I recognised what you were going through, Adam. I've been volunteering for the Samaritans on their phone lines for a while now, a couple of evenings a week.'

'So, in other words, you're a regular saint?'

She blew her cheeks out at me. 'I'm not sure about that. I just try to help people when I can. I'm certainly glad I was in the right place at the right time for you.' She glanced across at the queue of people at the drinks table. 'I'd better get back to it.' She paused and looked at me. 'There was one strange thing that night, though. You know you mentioned seeing a deer?'

'Yes?'

'Well, as I watched you leave, just for a moment I could have sworn I saw a doe ahead of you, but when I looked again she'd vanished.'

So someone else had witnessed it too. This was yet another strong piece of evidence that the doe hadn't simply been conjured up by my subconscious. But then again, I already knew that.

I smiled at her. 'Maybe my madness that night rubbed off on you a little bit.'

'Maybe…' She smiled and patted my arm, before heading back to the temporary bar.

I rejoined Sarah who was watching Matt still prowling around the cloth-covered object.

'The poor guy should try to relax,' I said.

'For someone so talented, he should have a bit more self-belief.'

'I know.' Sarah turned to me. 'So how are you doing, Adam? This isn't all proving too much for you?'

'Hopefully you can see for yourself?'

She did that Evie thing and tipped her head to one side to peer at me. 'Yes, much better. And I know how proud my sister would be if she could see you now.'

I noticed the robin watching me again and smiled to myself. 'I think you might be right about that.'

'I know I am,' Sarah said, clinking her glass against mine. Her gaze swept over the orchestra. 'I can't wait to hear her symphony. Do you know what Silvanus means?'

'Oh, it's very appropriate. Silvanus is the Roman god of the woods.'

'And that's appropriate because she was inspired to write the symphony here in Wytham?'

I gave her a broad smile. 'Something like that.'

The musicians began to tune their instruments.

Sarah leant in towards me. 'Have you got your notes for your speech, Adam?'

I shook my head. 'No, I'm just going to say what comes into my head – from my heart. I've been trying to do that a lot more these days.'

'That's good to hear.'

'It certainly feels like a much more authentic way to live my life.'

Sarah smiled and nodded.

Geoff pushed through the crowds, heading towards us. 'I think everybody's pretty much ready to get going when you are.'

I nodded and waved at Matt. 'Are you okay to do the big reveal once I've finished my speech?'

Matt paled. 'I guess so,' he called back, once again pulling at his shirt collar.

'Then let's get this show on the road,' Sarah said. She stuck her fingers in her mouth and blew a loud, ear-piercing whistle. All heads turned towards her. 'Okay, everyone, we're going to kick things off. To begin with Adam would like to say a few words.'

I took a sip of my orange juice to centre myself. Lilly and James gave me an encouraging look. I took a deep breath and began.

'Dear friends, I can't tell you what it means to me to see you all gathered here.' I gazed out at all the people standing under the trees. 'The tragedy is that Evie was stolen away from us far too soon. But here's the thing that took me a while to realise: she really isn't gone. She lives on within all our hearts.'

A lot of people nodded and Lilly put her hand to her chest as her eyes filled with tears.

'We all know that Evie was an exceptional woman and a seriously talented composer. In a moment we're going to hear the first public performance of Evie's *Silvanus Symphony*. And when you listen to it you'll hear Evie here too, her soul between the notes, where she'll live for ever...'

My voice caught but then I saw the robin flit over the heads of the crowd. It landed on one of Arwen's branches and bobbed its head at me as if it was encouraging me to go on.

I took a steadying breath before continuing. 'I was privileged to witness the birth of this symphony here beneath this very oak tree, which Evie and I nicknamed Arwen. And if I'm certain of anything, this music is destined to touch the hearts of many. The royalties earned from this piece will be given to a charity called

Evie's Eden. My wife believed in ecology as much as I do, so the plan is that some of the money raised will go towards a tree-planting scheme – a very active attempt to counter the deforestation happening on a global scale. Eventually I hope the charity will pay for experts to travel out to liaise with foresters around the world. They'll educate them about the role of mother trees and how they need to protect them from logging so that woodland habitats continue to thrive. I know this is something that Evie would have deeply approved of.'

Sarah looked at me with a smile and nodded.

'There is another strand to Evie's Eden – something very personal to me, since I lost my own way for a while. Many of you know how I struggled in the immediate months after Evie's death and I have to admit I was very close to giving up. In that time, I experienced two moments of genuine kindness. One was from a wonderful student of mine who made a crucial difference to me at a critical time.' I looked up and saw Christie beaming at me and gave her a smile back. 'The other was by a homeless guy who saw another human being in trouble: me. Sadly I haven't been able to track down this man to thank him, but he helped me in the one small way he could and I will always be grateful for that. In another life that homeless man could be any one of us standing here. Part of the charity's funds will be set aside to help the homeless of the world, people who have fallen out of society and live at the fringes, existing hand to mouth. They need our support and understanding. And I can tell you that someone in that situation needs all the help they can get.'

People nodded, clapped and whistled. I saw Lilly and James beaming.

I held up my hand and the applause faded away. 'And now I'd like to hand over to my best mate, Matt, an extremely talented artist. He's been working tirelessly on creating a fitting memorial of Evie.'

Matt nodded, slackened his tie and cleared his throat. 'I'm a man of few words—'

'If only!' Sarah called out.

A ripple of laughter ran through the audience.

Matt scraped his hand through his hair. 'Less heckling, you.'

Sarah grinned at him.

'Anyway, I've tried to create a piece that really captures the spirit of Evie. As you just heard, she shared Adam's passion for trees, so I hope she would have loved this. The title of this sculpture is quite simply "Evie", because that says everything.' Matt took hold of the cloth and pulled it off with a flourish.

The crowd gasped and tears filled my eyes.

Matt had not only excelled himself, he'd created something astonishing. The woman he'd carved from oak was the spitting image of Evie. But more importantly he'd really captured the essence of her. The figure had her arms thrown out, her head tipped back, her hair streaming into an invisible wind as she dissolved into a swirling pattern of leaves. It was utterly poetic and completely beautiful.

People were applauding and slapping Matt on the back as he pressed through the crowd towards Sarah and me.

'I hope you like it, Adam,' he said when he reached us.

'Mate, I love it.'

Tears blossomed in his eyes and he drew me into a tight bear hug, slapping me on the back.

When he finally let me go, Sarah grabbed him, giving him a big kiss. 'See, I told you everyone would love it!' She turned to the crowd and held up her glass. 'I'd like to raise a toast to Evie. She was an extraordinary woman who touched all our lives profoundly. And we'll never ever forget her.'

Everyone raised their glasses and replied, 'To Evie.'

Matt pulled his tie off and gestured towards Callum standing in front of the orchestra. 'Over to you now, buddy.'

Callum flicked his lion's mane of greying hair and nodded. He turned towards the musicians and stood perfectly still. There was complete silence, as though even the woods were waiting to hear the finished music.

Callum dipped his baton three times and the music began with a flute played by a female soloist. Her performance was as memorising and intoxicating as when I'd first heard Evie play here. And then the orchestra swelled around that single thread and it became something more: an entity given life by the talented musicians and their instruments. Evie's symphony soared among us, layered and exquisite.

Memory after memory surged through me – of Evie's love of life, of these woods, of her love for me. Hundreds of moments when she'd sparkled like a diamond. Many people in the audience were weeping now, but their eyes were wide with wonder too.

Sarah gently squeezed my arm. 'Oh my god,' she mouthed to me.

I nodded, smiling through my own tears. Sarah clung on to Matt's arm, his mouth hanging open as he listened.

The music continued to climb, taking everyone on an inward journey. It was then that I noticed a figure standing by Arwen. Everyone was so wrapped up in the music that no one noticed me heading over towards him.

I raised my hand in greeting. 'I'm glad you could make it, Silva.'

'Oh, I wouldn't have missed this for the world,' the old man replied. He held out a hand and I shook it.

I breathed in his familiar scent. 'I was wondering if I would ever see you again.'

'Just this one last time. There is something I need to tell you before I bid you farewell.'

'What is it?'

'It's simply this, Adam.' Silva gestured to the trees and then to my heart. 'Welcome home, my friend.'

I saw the doe watching me from farther off in the woods, her eyes gazing into my soul, of which she was already a part.

'Adam, are you okay?' I heard Sarah ask.

I glanced around to see her approaching. 'Yes, I'm fine. I'd like to introduce you to an old friend of mine.'

I turned back to Silva, but he had vanished, the doe too.

Sarah looked confused.

'Sorry, he must have slipped away. We should get back to the others and listen to the end of the symphony.'

Sarah nodded and linked her arm through mine as we walked together back towards the people whose hearts were being opened wide by the magic spell of Evie's music and would be forever changed.

AFTERWORD

You have just finished the most personal book I have ever written – and in many ways the most important one too.

The year I wrote the first draft this story – 2019 – was a harder year than most for me because of the loss of three very important people in my life.

We all have ways of grieving, but mine was perhaps more unusual than most. I tried to use their loss as a catalyst to do something positive and you're holding the result of that effort in your hands. *The Whisper of Trees* is a book that I'd been planning to write for years, but only now felt like the right moment for it to be born.

My intention was to write a story that might help someone who has lost a person close to them. If it helps even one struggling soul who's found themselves in a very dark place, then it'll have all been worth it. Ultimately *The Whisper of Trees* is a celebration of life and love.

I frequently had to dig deep when writing it. I read the first draft of it aloud to my wonderful wife, Karen, and a number of sequences in the story left us both in bits. The wedding vows that

Evie and Adam exchanged were based on our own and the Wytham wedding itself was basically our own wedding day transported to the middle of those woods.

About that magical woodland…

My study looks out across fields towards Wytham Woods, a place that Karen and I both adore. Research work really is carried out there by Oxford University. If you would like to visit it, you'll have to secure a permit first, but, oh my goodness, it is such a special place.

There are a number of main strands to *The Whisper of Trees*, some profound and others a heady mix of science and magic. Mycorrhizal networks are very real, as is the research work going on into them. The inclusion of them in this story was inspired by a fascinating TED Talk by Suzanne Simard, who was referenced in this story.

You can watch it here: https://www.ted.com/talks/suzanne_simard_how_trees_talk_to_each_other?language=en

The electrical impulses travelling between the trees are (very) loosely based on some articles I've read. I have no doubt stretched this idea beyond the point of scientific credibility, however this is a story after all and it is a plot device – as were Tolkien's talking Ents!

I have always had a strong affinity with trees and woodlands. As for Silva, I did in fact have my own slightly mystical experience when I was a teenager…

I was walking through an isolated stretch of woodland after a fresh fall of snow when I heard my name being called. This struck me as strange as the only way up to that wood was along the track I had used and I had seen no other footprints. A mysterious figure appeared out of the fog, heading towards me. Then it got really weird because he promptly vanished into thin air. To this day I cannot explain what exactly I encountered. Perhaps it was my own version of Silva! But being an author I wasn't going to waste it.

From this experience came the idea of a whisper heard in the woods, as did the character of Silva. The memory of that day has sat within me through all those years and it was that which influenced the more magical elements of this book. They certainly feel fitting as threads to weave around a scientist trying to make sense of the world and maybe they are a metaphor for my own internal struggle to reconcile the two.

Global warming caused by human action is a whole other subject in itself and I won't get into that here. However, if you feel inclined to do something practical to help, please consider donating to a charity such as the World Land Trust, who for £5 will plant a tree. You can find more information here: https://www.worldlandtrust.org/appeals/plant-a-tree/

Evie's music was always haunting as it floated around my head. I searched for something that might get close to help inspire me as I wrote this book. I found that flash of inspiration eventually among the works of Max Richter and specifically his track entitled 'On the Nature of Daylight', which frequently leaves me in tears when I listen to it. The track builds to something that really does speak to my soul and I hope it does for you too.

You can listen to a live performance of 'On the Nature of Daylight' on YouTube here (you can also find it on music streaming apps such as Spotify and iTunes): https://www.youtube.com/watch?v=b_YHE4Sx-08

In this book I've briefly touched upon the plight of the homeless. When we see a homeless person on the street, we usually have no idea of what led them to living such a life. With a flip of the dice, that might be us watching strangers hurry by and avoiding eye contact. There is always more that can be done for people in these situations. If you are considering making a donation to help them, please do. There are many charities to choose from – in the UK, I recommend Shelter: https://www.shelter.org.uk

As for the cancer story thread, that's something I know a bit about. It's time for me to admit something very personal to you. I was diagnosed with chronic leukaemia three years ago. For those less familiar with CLL, as it's known, it's not as serious as the acute version that Evie had. It's what's considered to be one of the *good* cancers. I have a strong fighting chance of living to an old age and I have every intention of doing so. However, I also had a second scare last year when doctors found I had very early stage-one cancer cells during a routine bowel check-up. These were successfully removed and I'm monitored regularly to make sure I'm okay. But if I hadn't had that first check-up from which my chronic leukaemia was discovered, and it had been left for another couple of years, it would have been a very different story. My life was saved by the NHS and I will eternally be grateful to the dedicated people who work in that incredible organisation. Please do always attend your health screening check-ups because they might just save your life too. I have always led a very healthy lifestyle, but since my diagnosis I've made some tweaks that I hope will make a significant difference in the years ahead.

All this certainly made me suddenly very aware of my own mortality and that the clock was most definitely ticking. That's another of the many reasons why I had to write *The Whisper of Trees* now.

I feel very fortunate, since I am incredibly happy, full of energy and married to my very own Evie in the form of Karen, who lights up each and every day of my life. I feel blessed to be on this journey called life and intend to make the most of it. But while we might always strive to seize the day, sometimes those who mean everything to us can be stolen away far too soon. And I have lost too many people, specifically to cancer, recently. The heartache of loss is one of the hardest things to endure.

Three core messages around this theme exist in *The Whisper of Trees*...and they are old truths that you will have heard many times over.

The first is that in my experience we really do carry those we love in our hearts. Who we surround ourselves with becomes part of who we are – that magical connection with another human being.

The second message is that life truly is a gift and to use your time on this planet as the precious thing that it is. I try to avoid wasting time staring into the seductive black mirror of a mobile phone and spend more time living the life I have been gifted. Astronomy has always been one of my passions and I can tell you that the statistical chances of being born as a human being on Earth – a rare M-class planet that can sustain life – is incredibly infinitesimal, so please don't squander the time that you have.

My final message is about the nature of loss itself and this is the central reason why I wrote this book. I've written this especially for anyone recently bereaved. There is a truth important to hang on to during the painful process of grieving: that time really is a healer. I believe in taking each day as it comes, placing one foot in front of another and keeping going. Anyone grieving will have good days and bad days, but will start to surface and be able turn their face to the sun to feel its warmth again one day. If you're hurting, please don't shut yourself away. Reach out. Human contact is vital at a time like this. Certainly don't wait until it's too late. If all you can see are black dogs, then reach out to an organisation that will be able to help, such as the Samaritans in the UK: https://www.samaritans.org

As I look up from my keyboard and through the study window, I can see the final leaves of autumn lying in golden piles on the ground as winter takes hold of this year. But soon, those same trees will be sprouting the fresh green leaves of spring. If you want a metaphor for life, that's it right there: an endless cycle of stardust being constantly reborn and reformed. An end is not an end. So I say that while we're here we should make sure to leave our footprints in the sand, helping to make the world a slightly better place than the one we found. I can think of no better way to honour the memory of those we have lost than that.

Nicholas Cook, November 2019 (written on my birthday)

LINKS

Do please leave that all important review for ***The Whisper of Trees*** here: https://geni.us/TheWhisperOfTrees

Printed in Great Britain
by Amazon

54874276R00137